T0208360

In The Land Of Cane

And Other Selected Work

M.D. SHANNON

iUniverse, Inc.
New York   Bloomington

In The Land Of Cane
And Other Selected Work

iUniverse books may be ordered through booksellers or by contacting:

iUniverse
1663 Liberty Drive
Bloomington, IN 47403
www.iuniverse.com
1-800-Authors (1-800-288-4677)

Because of the dynamic nature of the Internet, any Web addresses or links contained in this book may have changed since publication and may no longer be valid. The views expressed in this work are solely those of the author and do not necessarily reflect the views of the publisher, and the publisher hereby disclaims any responsibility for them.

ISBN: 978-1-4502-2387-4 (sc)
ISBN: 978-1-4502-2388-1 (ebk)

Printed in the United States of America

iUniverse rev. date: 4/23/2010

DEDICATED TO

KAREN, KARLA, AND MARIA

Contents

FOREWORD

M.D. Shannon grew up in the Upper Gulf Coast region of Texas. While still a child, his father (note 1) began to suffer bouts of schizophrenia, and his mother, seeing her husband was unable to care for their three children, took up roots and moved to Philadelphia. The sixties were a turbulent era in America, and the effects were profoundly felt in the inner-cities; drugs, crime, and violence were the dark hallmarks of a generation. Surviving such turmoil while so many others perished, Shannon made his way back to the Gulf Coast region where he graduated from The University of Texas with a degree in the performance literature.

Aspiring to become a poet/playwright, he traveled to Mexico and began to write. He taught school, got married and started a family. During this period, he wrote numerous poems and short plays, but his work was lost, and all that remains is a few poems. Returning to the U.S. in the 1980's, he enrolled in graduate school. However, after a year of coursework and research, he became disillusioned with academia. He then took up various occupations ranging from teaching to entrepreneurship. Regarding his business acumen, he was a poor manager of finances, and if not for the frequent mortgaging of his home, and also his father who had inherited his brother's estate (note 2), he would have gone broke on more than a few occasions.

By the 1990's, his father had recovered somewhat from his illness, and the writer as finally able to get to know him, which is something he always longed for, but he was unable to do because of his father's affliction. He was intrigued to learn that his father had a secret fondness for literature, especially poetry, and that he had committed to memory a number of poems, often reciting them to the delight of his son.

While a desire to write remained, it was more than a decade before Shannon would lift up the pen. He turned his attention to trade writing, and in a period of five years he created two novels, a modern libretto, and an international screenplay. Throughout the period he tried to find recognition for his work, but he was unsuccessful. However, his failure did not keep him from writing, and he persisted, though it became clear he was in danger of sacrificing his health and the welfare of his family. Tragedy soon stepped in, and he fell ill with a serious liver condition. The diagnosis was end-stage sclerosis with complication of edema and encephalitis. Such complications are often fatal, and at an early point of his illness, he was given two weeks to make it. He did, however, get through the critical period by attaining the best medical care available (note 3), maintaining a radically altered diet, and basically refusing to give up the ghost.

The agonized years leading to his recovery were compounded with dread, for he was plagued both physically and mentally. In one of his personal letters, he refers to his "pale mirror-reflection that reveals a dead soul," and to "ashen flesh and lifeless sinew.....a shallow, nightmarish body that once housed a vigorous man and a vital dream."

The symptoms of advanced sclerosis are horrific in appearance, but the accompanying psychological conditions can be much worse. A confrontation with one's mortality is a conflict that many find impossible to overcome; however, when once achieved, it brings the possibility of a new beginning.

Nearly five years passed before M.D. Shannon's health improved enough to allow him to effectively write. The stories he chooses to create are not sated with suffering as one might suspect from a writer who endured so much, but rather they are infused with hope, and perseverance. His characters, though, are often a myriad of contradictions. They speak to our humanness; of both darkness and light, of weakness and strength, of success and failure. Despite such conflict, the message of his work is abundantly clear. Life is necessarily cast in suffering, but it need not be a hopeless affliction, for anguish can be an instrument of change, a purveyor of knowledge and transcendence.

Autumn, 2009

PART ONE: A NOVEL

IN THE LAND OF CANE

This fictional novel parallels actual events that occurred following the Civil War when Afro-American were forced to labor (note 4) in the vast sugarcane fields of the upper Gulf Coast region of Texas.

PROLOGUE

The river was smooth and it wound murkily, rising with the seasonal rains and receding with the dry ones, laggardly moving, like a serpent on the sly, cutting the face of the land with its body, shaping banks and inlets for miles, creating the land that would one day become Magnolia, and later Sugarville, and now a story for us all. For the land is a dwelling place of spirit, and as such, it is a shared place of souls, existing everywhere in the geography of heaven, which is timeless, but also now, becoming ours to shape and imagine, as it was long ago by angels and demons who, empowered by light and darkness, trod the earth with will.

1.

Wilkie James, a youthful Afro American, strolled along a dusty orchard road in Georgia, his bare feet stepping light-footed, his taunt arms merrily swinging as crows cawed on the branches of trees overhead. Field hands in the distance sang songs of the harvest season, and their melodies drifted above the trees while sunrays beamed down from heaven, bringing luster and warmth to the land.

After three miles of walking, Wilkie came to the tiny town of Jefferson. Sauntering passed the sheriff's office, he bid good-day to a group of old red-necks who sat on the porch smoking cigars and drinking liquor. Entering the town's general store, he stepped up to the counter and set down a pair of shiny nickels.

"Corn meal and sugar," he said to Elmer Smithy, the store's owner, and the town's volunteer deputy. Elmer weighed out the appropriate amounts on a tin scale. Bagging up the sugar and the meal, he handed two small sacks to Wilkie, who then slipped the sacks inside his shirt.

Elmer noticed that Wilkie's shirt bulged open, and other items were inside it. "What else you got inside that shirt, boy?" he asked.

Wilkie delightfully reached inside his shirt and lifted out a peach for Elmer to see. "They's peaches," he replied. "Sweet, ripe Georgia peaches."

"Where'd you get 'em, boy?"

"I picks 'em up on the orchard road. Harvest season come early this year. Peaches layin' here and there. No sense in lettin' crows have 'em."

Elmer cocked an eye and rubbed a stubble of beard on his chin. "You been thievin' from the McCall Orchard, ain't ya boy? Your mama teach you no better?"

"No sir, I been thievin' nothin'. Like I says, peaches everywhere on the road."

Elmer stepped around the counter and spoke to Wilkie with an air of authority. "Come along, boy. We'll see what the sheriff wants to do about this."

Wilkie shrugged his shoulders, and he walked languidly toward the sheriff's office, Elmer following closely behind him.

2.

In spring of 1870, Confederate Captain Addison McGeary traveled by wagon into old Magnolia Plantation, having recently become the proud owner of thirty square miles of lowlands in the central Gulf Coast region. Nothing of the plantation town remained, except for a deep-water well, and a few drinking troughs for animals. Most people in the region scoffed at what seemed an imprudent purchase, but McGeary knew what he had, and not merely for the Snake River that ran through his land, but for an abandoned frontier fort the Confederates had used as a prison. Slavery now abolished, plantations were going belly up everywhere, and McGeary, perceiving the importance of acquiring a new class of the indentured, wisely gifted the prison to the state along with five-hundred acres of rich farm land. In exchange, he received leasing rights to state convicts, effectively making him an important player in the emerging industry of convict labor.

A tall, handsome figure, McGeary's most distinguishing feature was an earthy-red beard, which he wore perennially tangled and matted. The only exception was during his trips down river to Coastal City where, after a bath and a grooming, he would don a suit, and a collar studded with silver. He'd then binge on bourbon, poker and women, sometimes for weeks.

Throughout his early years in Magnolia, people said McGeary was odious, working his convicts for long hours in the fields, and even extending their sentences a few weeks to conform to harvest season. But the truth is, whatever else he was, he was also a compassionate man, for he built two-room houses for the families of his convicts, allowing the families to live near their loved ones.

Magnolia flourished by the cultivation of sugarcane. Cane grew hardily in the lush lowlands, and it was easily marketed. McGeary constructed a mammoth sugar mill among a host of smaller ones, and he had plans to build a local rail line, which he believed would one day connect with the Midwest Southern Rail Road and make Magnolia the most important source of sugar in the south.

As Magnolia grew and became profitable, convicts reaped the benefits of its success. Trusted convicts were allowed to live with their families in the houses that McGeary built, and after they served their sentences, many stayed on and continued working, but now on a salaried basis. This transition from convict to citizen was a social dynamic that helped Magnolia grow into a town. Road and water converged here, spurning warehouses, smiths and stables, all teeming with mosquitoes and permeated with the smoke from the mills. It was not an idyllic existence, but it was far better than prison life, and it held the promise of opportunity as well.

3.

In 1879 the area surrounding Magnolia had a free population of nearly six hundred, mostly blacks, a white minority, and a few Hispanics and Asians. The state granted the region a charter that year and South Fort County was created. Local government was founded, and an austere courthouse was built. White landowners in the new county were appointed to official positions, and all went smoothly for awhile. Then election time came around, and black citizens began to lobby for representation. On the day of election, much to the white's chagrin, black candidates won a decisive victory. Talk began to circulate about what to do.

"We're gonna get rid of 'em," declared Lucien Eliot, a lean, blond landowner with beady eyes. Fond of pointed-toe boots and vaquero hats, he resided with an aura of the American west. "I won't stand for uppity coloreds," he said, his hands haughtily grasping his hips as he strutted through a crowd of white men. "No matter they's elected."

Captain McGeary was the only man with the courage to disagree with Lucien. "I see no cause fer blood. I don't want my land stained by the killin' of men, colored or white."

Lucien gazed at McGeary with a baneful eye. "I imagine some men don't have a stomach for killin'."

A young man stepped through the crowd and appeared in the midst of the two landowners. He was McGeary's adopted son, Andrew, a pale, high-strung soul whom McGeary found in Tucson begging on the streets. Andrew's parents had died of consumption, and McGeary, having pity for the ten-year-old orphan, took him in.

"I'll do what needs be done," Andrew proudly told Lucien. "I ain't never kilt a man before, but most folks say coloreds ain't human. So maybe killin' one or two ain't so bad."

McGeary pulled Andrew aside. "Son, there won't be killin' by me or by you. We all know coloreds ain't equal to whites, but murdering a man is murder all the same."

"I never was like you," Andrew confessed, his eyes falling away to the ground. "I don't see nothin' wrong with killin'."

McGeary's countenance grew stormy. "I've had you looked after all your life," he declared. "I tried to raise you right, and I always got you whatever you want."

"Maybe gettin' rid of the coloreds is what I want," said Andrew. "Maybe killin' won't bother me like it does you."

Captain McGeary's eyes glared behind his beard, his ire building as tension mounted. "Boy, you don't know what you're talkin'."

Andrew was undeterred by his father's anger. "I hear the stories. Nobody says you was a coward fightin' the Yankees, only that you stayed out of the fightin' whene'er you could."

Captain McGeary grasped Andrew's shoulders, forcing his son to peer up into his eyes. "You go on, boy," he ordered. "If killin' is want you want, then I imagine the world's got a place for you. For my part, though, I've seen enough death."

4.

Stuffing his wallet with twelve-hundred dollars in cash, Captain McGeary traveled down river to Coastal City. He didn't bother with a bath when he arrived, but went directly to the saloon. Cradling a bottle of bourbon, he eased into a poker game and proceeded to win seven consecutive hands, three on a bluff. Filling his glass to the brim, he took a long, hard drink. Then gradually standing erect, he announced, "I'll be back."

No one at the table objected. They merely watched as the red-bearded man stacked his winnings into a pair of neat piles, and, folding up the bills with his big hands, he inserted them deep into the pockets of his trousers. Stumbling upstairs to the second floor, he found a familiar door and passed through it. Beatrice Baudelaire, a fair, finely sculptured French woman with an impeccable facility for language, stood behind the half wall of her boudoir. Strapping on a garter, she was naked from the waist up.

"Mousier McGeary," Beatrice intoned. "I did not expect you so soooon."

McGeary set his bottle on her dresser with a clunk. The sound caused Beatrice to take notice, and she peered curiously at her guest. He stood motionless, except for his head, which weaved ever so slightly, moving up and down and sideways, searching for the proper degrees by which to fix his gaze and to steady his world. Beatrice realized the big man might fall away, and crossing over to him, she steadied his body by hugging his waist.

"I'll be a'right," McGeary said surly.

Beatrice turned her attention to the bed, and gently drew back a cotton blanket to expose a silk sheet and a pair of duck-feather pillows. She fluffed the pillows with her hands, then she smoothed the sheets with delicate strokes of her fingers, much like a Goddess would in preparing an immaculate bed for an immortal. She then took McGeary by the hand and drew him to the edge of the bed, where, dropping to the floor, she knelt at his feet and unloosened the laces of his boots. McGeary got the message, and he responded by lifting up his legs. She removed one boot, then the other, setting each carefully aside as though they were fine garments. When McGeary felt himself bootless, he fell back, his arms spread lengthwise across the bed, and his eyelids drawn down heavily over his eyeballs. As he lay, he got the sensation of her hands working to undo his shirt and belt. Suddenly, he felt a tug as she drew his trousers off his legs. He fell into a dream before Beatrice could remove his shirt. She therefore allowed him to lie in peace, sleeping in his fallen place, smelling of liquor, breathing in rhythm with the breeze.

Beatrice reached into McGeary's trousers' pocket and removed the cash. After a cursory inspection, she estimated its worth at nearly three-thousand dollars. She rolled off a pair of one-hundred-dollar bills for herself and slipped them into her brazier. The remaining cash she stashed behind a loose board in the wall.

A knock came to the door and Beatrice answered. It was Cassandra, an island-woman. Like nearly everyone in Coastal City, Cassandra had a hard-luck story. Her husband had practiced sorcery, and the authorities forced him to flee the mainland, leaving his wife to her own devices, which included the making of secret potions.

"He back, hu?" Cassandra asked, peering at McGeary on the bed. "I knew. Didn't think so soon, though. I put a spell on him. He a good man, but he know too much sin. I told him so, about the land too. The war change things. Some land clean. No man, though." She pushed back the braids of her hair and leaned over the bed. Putting her face close to McGeary's, she smelled his breath. "Bourbon?" Cassandra guessed. "He gamble yet?"

"Yes," Beatrice replied.

Cassandra grinned, exposing a broken tooth at the front of her mouth. "He got money?" she asked.

"I imagine you need some," Beatrice replied.

"Even the devil need money," the island woman commented.

Beatrice reached into a drawer and withdrew a gold coin. "Here's ten dollars," she said, handing the coin to Cassandra. "Wash his trousers and bring them back nicely pressed."

"I do that," Cassandra said richly. "Sure do."

5.

McGeary slept soundly, and he did not awaken until mid-morning. He was a voracious handler of a knife and fork, but on this occasion, when Cassandra brought him a breakfast of eggs, beans and beefsteak, he was unenthused.

"I had me a dream," he said, poking the beefsteak with his fork somberly. "The same as years ago."

"What was it?" Cassandra asked. "You wanna talk 'bout it? I knows about such things."

McGeary thought of his dream, and he revisited images of red rain flowing ribbon-like from the sky. The rain filled the fields with crimson, and the earth's rivers ran coldly with the color of blood. "Ain't nothin' a man wants to share," he explained. "Some things best be lived with alone." He pushed away his plate. "It was a sign, though," he commented. "That's for sure. I best sell."

Beatrice overheard, and stepping away from her dresser mirror, she asked McGeary, "sell your land?"

"I'll find a decent buyer," McGeary replied. "Many's a wantin' cane. We'll move west. California. Land flows of milk and honey. Not like here."

"Land flows wit' blood in these parts," Cassandra commented. "Gots to. Like a woman some land is."

"Hush!" Beatrice admonished. "It's not polite to talk like that."

"Maybe," Cassandra agreed. "It's the truth, though."

McGeary stood and stepped into his trousers. "Think I'll play some poker," he announced. "Give the boys a chance to win some of their money back."

"Not yet," said Beatrice, taking McGeary by the arm. "Walk with me through town and down by the water."

"That's right," Cassandra concurred. "Too soon after a dream like that. You best walk in the salt air."

Beatrice guided Captain McGeary outdoors. She strolled with him along the sidewalks of town, showing him off like a prize. The time had come, she cheerfully thought. Captain McGeary would finally take her away. She held her head loftily in the morning air, her eyes searching the porches of affluent homes, desiring for the town's respectable ladies to catch sight of her with the rich landowner.

The couple summoned a carriage and traveled down to the water. The beach was empty, except for broken seashells and strutting droves of gulls. The moon was away, and the tide was peaceful, crawling lazily ashore, and washing the sand with clear, calm strokes.

6.

Two dissimilar yet equally affected storms brewed upon the land of South Fort County, one in the minds of men and the other in the soul of the sky. Both hellacious and damning, they came together not by accident, but by the mood of the moon, which was waxing full and incandescent. The storm of the sky had been building on the horizon for hours, but only when the storm of men congealed did it fully manifest itself and demonstrate its powers. The storms began with the appearance of low-hanging clouds, and the wind swirling, uplifting the leaves of trees, causing small animals of the fields to seek shelter in hovels. The land was quiet, except for the stalks of cane, which rustled in the wind, murmuring a dialog of inextricable nature. Yet everyone who passed along the field that evening understood the intention of the storm, and too the moon, which appeared in gaps between turbulent clouds, giving evidence to a dreadful transit that had come to the land.

A mile away from the South Fort Courthouse, Lucien Eliot rode with a band of twenty men, all of them armed with weapons, their horses galloping steadily, their hoofs thundering the ground, like drums of an ancient order. Drops of rain fell from the sky, large ones stinging skin, and making rude, slapping sounds on leather. The heavens crackled with lightning, and it riled the horses, but they remained apace and in concert, for the animals sucked moist air into their nostrils, the fresh, watery scent exhilarating them.

Inside the courthouse, seven blacks newly elected to office had taken refuge. Whites had told the blacks to relinquish their rights and to leave the county by nightfall. Believing the courthouse their protector, the blacks locked themselves inside. None was armed, except for the pocket knives some men carried. However, at the rear of the building was the sheriff's office, and it was laden with weapons.

"You don't knows what yer getting into," the county sheriff informed the black men. A bulky lawman, he rarely carried a weapon, but on this occasion he wore a pistol. A forward-thinking man, his usual weapon of choice was the instrument of straight talk. "You must think Lucien is a comin' here to negotiate. Well, he ain't."

Henry Fields, a mature, educated black man, stepped forward. His gray hair framed the corners of his face, making him appear distinguished. "We know our rights," he declared, a roll of legal papers in his hand. "This is our county as much as anybody's."

Henry could read and write better than most whites in South Fort County. For this reason, he was well-respected among his peers, but white men merely found him a curious anomaly.

The sheriff stepped up into Henry's face. "You think cause you been to school you got somethin'," he began. "Oh, sure, you got things in yer head, but you don't have a white color skin."

His words seemed to shame the crowd of black men, for they hung back silently.

"We're free men," Lucas Brown spoke up abruptly. The youngest man in the group, he had not known the days of slavery first-hand, but he knew quite well the oppression of present days. His father died one August afternoon of God-knows-what while working the sugar fields. Some say it was it was exhaustion, others say it was a blow to the head. "The Federals knows about this," Lucas added. "They's on the way. They'll put things right and give us what's ours."

The sheriff mumbled like an old cynic, and then he distinctly spoke. "Yeah, well, the Federals won't be here for two days," he explained. "Lucien is armed. You're not. He won't burn the courthouse down. He'll light it with lead. Best get out whilst you got a chance."

"You're the sheriff!" a voice cried out from the crowd. "You're supposed to protect the people!"

It was the sheriff's turn to be ashamed. "I can only do what I can do," he confessed. In the distance, the sound of galloping horses climbed above the wind. The sheriff listened and let out a pitiful sigh. "You folks stay back. I'll talk with Lucien." Peering out from on the porch, the sheriff saw a red sky looming behind Lucien's men as they rode in. With rifles propped on their saddles, they looked as ominous as the riotous clouds thronging overhead, for both were menacing and glazed with fury.

Lucien drew up to the courthouse in lead of the group. "Step aside," he ordered the lawman. "Don't cause no trouble."

The sheriff stood with his arms folded across his chest. It was not so much a demonstration of defiance as it was a gesture indicating his unwillingness to touch the revolver he wore on his hip. "They's free men, Lucien. They gots rights like everybody else."

"Is that what the County Sheriff says?"

"It's what the coloreds say. But I'm sheriff and sworn to uphold the law."

Lucien grinned. "You're appointed to the office, aren't you? Appointed by me and the men here, right?"

"That's right."

"And beings you's appointed, you can be un-appointed."

"I imagine so."

"Then consider yerself un-appointed as sheriff. Step off the porch. Get on your buggy and head on home. Yer wife's got dinner waitin'."

The white men hooted and hollered, beguiling the sheriff, who, seeing no alternative, stepped off the courthouse porch and marched toward his buggy.

Lucien fashioned a sardonic smile. "I like a man who thinks with his stomach," he proclaimed. "It's the kind of fella you can trust."

Gray-haired Henry Fields peaked out a second-floor window of the courthouse, trying to discern the on-goings. "Sheriff's going out on his buggy," he announced. "We're all to ourselves now."

"What we gonna do?"

"We can act like free men, or high-tail and run."

"If we act like free men, we'll be dead men."

"Lucien will kill us, that's fer sure."

"He won't kill the seven of us."

"We ain't even armed."

Talk continued among the black men, and it abated only when Lucien brazenly stepped onto the courthouse porch and shouted through a half-open door. "We give you folks a chance!" he barked. "Come on out! We'll see you get home safely. You all got families. Best think of them than anything else."

Henry stood at the top of the courthouse stairs and shouted down. "Some want to come out and others don't!"

Lucien mulled over a reply before responding. "Send out the ones who want!"

Moments later, five black men walked out of the courthouse, only Lucas Brown and Henry remained inside. It had yet to begin to rain, but the vespers of evening had descended, and twilight bore shades of amber and violet. The sight would have been a splendid marvel of nature if not for the inglorious reality that occurred thereafter: a group of white men encircled the five blacks, and closing in, they snickered and mocked them.

"We don't wants no trouble," said Jupiter, a long-suffering ex-convict who had worked McGeary's cane fields as a free man for five years. "You said you'd see us safely home."

"Oh, we gonna see ya home," a white man said laughing. "Only it ain't gonna be to no shanty. We gonna see you home to The Promise Land."

Inside the courthouse, young Lucas nudged the more-experienced Henry. "What you think they's gonna do?" Lucas asked.

"They'll kill them," replied Henry. "Just like they'll kill us if we don't do something."

Henry marched downstairs and Lucas followed. Entering the sheriff's office, they selected weapons in silence. They spoke nothing, nor did they peer into one another's eyes. Perhaps it was fear for what they might see. Perhaps it was an unwillingness to say good-bye. Bearing rifles, they took positions at windows. It was dim outdoors now, but Henry and Lucas could discern the movements of men and horses. They watched as Lucien and his men shifted back to an area beneath a group of trees, where brandishing pistols they held the five black men in check. One of the whites swung a rope over a low-hanging branch and began to fashion a noose with his hands. A pair of white men pushed a black man onto a saddle, but the horse rejected the actions and kicked one of the men in the shoulder, causing him to stumble backward. A shot abruptly rang out from a courthouse window, and it grazed a white man's forehead. He fell from his mount and hit the ground with a thud. The others scrambled for cover.

"What in heaven's name are you trying to do?" cried Henry.

"I ain't gonna watch our friends die!" Lucas exclaimed.

The black man on the horse dashed off, clinging to the horse's mane like a kid. The other blacks scurried into a cane field, and after separating, they ran for miles in disparate directions.

Once the fog of confusion lifted, Andrew and three friends pursued the fleeing men. After riding for nearly an hour, the group slipped into a cane field and came upon a pair of blacks, finding them lying low on the grubby ground. One of the men was Jupiter, and the other was his friend, Elias, a headstrong man known for his resolve and courage.

Andrew hooted and hollered. "Get up and run! We gives you a chance."

Elias stood up. "We're tired of running."

"Then we'll shoot ya here," Andrew declared. He got down from his horse and drew his pistol, pointing it in the face of Elias. "You want it first?"

Elias didn't flinch. "You just gonna murder us?" he asked.

"Sure, why not?" replied a white, laughing with his cohorts.

Elias pulled a knife from his trouser pocket and expertly wielded the blade. "Maybe it's best we fight!" he cried.

Andrew grinned. "I knows somethin' about knife fightin' too." He withdrew a dagger from his belt, and held it high.

With Elias's eyes fixed on Andrew's knife, he circled in measured steps, like an animal stalking its prey. But it was Andrew who struck first, letting blood by slashing Elias' hand.

"You won't do that no mo'," Elias promised.

The black man leapt at McGeary and the two began to tussle, their blades slicing the air in violent strokes. The fighters appeared evenly matched, for neither man's knife could find a deadly mark and fell the other. But Elias stood the better ground, and soon he swiped at Andrew's neck and nicked it. Andrew saw this as an opportunity, and he went up with his blade, catching Elias in the chest and cracking his rib. The wounded man dropped his knife and stood dizzily, his eyes rolling in his head. Once he fell backward, Andrew proclaimed Elias dead.

"You see that?!" cried Andrew. "I got him in the chest! Cut his heart, I bet". He removed a tobacco from his shirt pocket and lit it, adrenalin pumping in his veins.

"He went down like a rock! I kilt that colored with a single stroke!" He sucked heartily on his tobacco and exhaled. The white men were aghast, for Elias had opened a gash on Andrew's throat and smoke flowed out of it, like through a pair of grotesque lips.

Andrew's friends helped him sit as blood streamed from the wound on his neck. They tried to inhibit the bleeding, but they could do little keep the blood from backing up and filling the cavity of Andrew's throat. Andrew began to choke, at first mildly, then with intensity. He was dead within minutes. His friends did not bother to search for Jupiter. They simply mounted their horses and galloped for home.

7.

The wind commanded the battleground at the courthouse rather than the rain. It chilled the spirit and disturbed the mind, moving nosily among the trees, slashing at branches and striping off leaves. Some leaves fell to the ground and stumbled away, while others took flight with tumultuous wings, spinning in the coils of the storm. Lucas and Henry, though, were no longer cognizant of the turbulence, for they were inside the courthouse strategizing their next move.

"Maybe we can escape," Henry said. "But we need to know where Lucien is."

"That means gettin' in the ravine," responded Lucas.

"Yeah," Henry agreed.

The two men slipped out a rear window of the courthouse and ran through the rain until they found the ravine. Creeping on all fours, they crawled through muddy water.

Meanwhile, waiting in the shadows of the trees, Lucien grew impatient. "You men watch the courthouse," he ordered. "If you see a Negro, shoot 'em." Crouching down, Lucien stepped stealthily toward the courthouse steps, his eyes surveying the ground before him. Suddenly, he heard a boom, which at first he believed was thunder. But pain pierced his shoulder, and he realized a bullet struck him.

"That you, Lucien?" a voice asked from behind an oak near the courthouse. The voice belonged to Stump, called so for his stockiness.

"Yeah, it's me," replied Lucien.

"Didn't hit ya, did I?" Stump asked.

"Yeah, ya did," Lucien replied.

"I figured you for a colored," Stump confessed.

A long moment passed before Lucien asked, "where are they?"

"I don't know," Stump replied. "I can't see nothin' through the trees."

Lucien waddled cautiously over to the place where Stump was hiding. When he caught his breath, he said, "you didn't shoot me so bad. Could a killed me, though." Stump thought it best to not comment. "We gotta know where the Negroes are," Lucien continued. "So, you gots to get out in the open."

"I might git killed out there!" Stump objected.

"Coloreds can't hit an ol' stump like you," said Lucien. "Yer too damn short."

Stump was reluctant, but Lucien wielded power over his friends in the same manner he did his field hands. He cajoled and threatened them, and when that didn't work, they were brutally punished. Stump stepped out into the open, pacing over wet gravel, unnerved by the groveling beneath his feet. When he passed near a window of the courthouse, he began to run, scampering clumsily like a bug. Finding a fat tree trunk, he got safely behind it.

"I didn't see nothing!" Stump called out to Lucien.

"Maybe they's in the ravine!" Lucien shouted back. "Best you come back this way!"

Stump felt like crying out *hell no!* But he didn't dare. He came out into full view once more, but this time he moved rapidly, not caring he stepped noisily. Finding Lucien, he sat down in the wet grass beside him. "What are we gonna do now?" Stump asked.

Lucien pondered the question. "Best we head on home," he replied. "We'll find them tomorrow."

In the ravine, Henry and Lucas pressed on in search for Lucien and his men. The rain had slowed now, and the ground was quiet, but it did not decrease the anxiety that rankled the air. Henry, the more experienced man, peered back over his shoulder and saw Lucas stalled on all fours.

"What is it?" asked Henry, trying to keep his voice soft but still loud enough to be heard.

Lucas said nothing, but the bulge in his eyes said he saw something frightening. Henry looked about, and he noticed a snake in the water. Curved in three places, its long, black back exposed its body, like a grand sea serpent. Gliding in the water, the snake raised its head and stared at Lucas with piercing, caliginous eyes.

"It's only a dang water snake," Henry informed his friend.

Lucas ignored his words, and pressing his hands to his face, he shielded himself from the serpent, which, apparently disinterested in Lucas, slithered off, its body rippling through water.

"It was a cotton mouth," Lucas claimed, after the snake was out of sight. "Had it bit me, I'd be dead. You couldn't see what it was, but I could."

"Oh, I saw all right," Henry responded. "I knew it was a cotton mouth. But what could I say?"

"You could have said," Lucas uttered nervously. "You could have said—oh, nothing. Just forget it ever happened."

Rounding a bend in the ravine, the two men discovered they had journeyed more than two-hundred yards. However, there was no sign of Lucien or his men anywhere. Henry and Lucas realized they were gone.

"What do you think of that?" asked Lucas, slapping a puddle delightfully with his hand. "They high-tailed and run off."

"Don't know what to think," said Henry. "One thing for sure, though. We best get home, take what's ours and leave the county. Lucien will want us dead—that's for certain."

8.

Three miles out from the courthouse, Lucien, riding with six shadowy forms, returned to pass along the fields, to the place where the moon had swept earlier that evening, where the wind had whispered with the stalks of cane. The sky merely drizzled now. The horses were exhausted and spent. They paced laggardly, their necks bent, and their eyes downcast. They reached a stone bridge on a creek between Lucien's and McGeary's land. The animals drank water, and the men washed mud from their faces and hands. The clouds cleared, and they graciously opened a place for the moon. Moonlight reflected down on the water, dancing in radiant ripples.

The outline of a man appeared downstream. It was Jupiter, traipsing through shallow creek-water. He entered a cane field like a phantom and journeyed deep into it.

Lucien noticed Jupiter's ghostly movements, and he pursued him. "You was one of the coloreds that run off," Lucien said, drawing up to Jupiter. "Where's the others?"

"Elias is dead," Jupiter replied. "Don't know 'bout the others."

"Who kilt him?" Lucien quizzed,

"Young McGeary," answered Jupiter.

"And where's young McGeary?" asked Lucien.

"I don't know," replied Jupiter. "When they got to fightin' with knives, I run off."

"Don't lie," Lucien commanded. "I want the truth. You know me. You know what I can do."

Jupiter hung his head. "Young McGeary dead, too," he said sickly. "Cut with a knife."

Lucien dropped a rope over Jupiter's shoulders and tightened it at his midsection. He dragged him out of the field and through the water of the creek. On the road, he found a tree, and here he drew Jupiter up. Not bothering to place a knotted rope about Jupiter's neck, Lucien simply put a bullet in him, leaving him to spin with the rain and wind; that is until morning, when a trio of black women arrived, and after cutting Jupiter down, they buried him in a shale grave near a bend in the creek.

9.

Andrew McGeary was laid to rest on a hill overlooking the Snake River. Captain McGeary spoke little after his son's burial, but he got word out that he was ready to sell his land. Everyone figured he was hurt so badly by the tragedy of his son that he would take most any offer. Lucien Eliot was interested in McGeary's land, and he made arrangement to submit a reasonable bid.

It was during a humid hour following a brief rain that the two men got together at McGeary's place. Lucien plunged into business without as much as a greeting.

"That's my offer," he said, setting a muddy boot upon the steps of McGeary's porch. "Take the money and move to California. Start a new life fer yerself. Two-hundred and thirty-thousand dollars is a lot of money. You bought the place for a fraction of that."

Lucien was known to be a tough negotiator, but McGeary was hardly a push-over. "It don't matter what it *was* worth back then," McGeary said. "Only what it's worth now. If two-hundred and thirty-thousand is all you got to offer, then get along and leave me to my bereavement."

"It's a good offer," Lucien objected. "Hard, cold cash."

"It ain't a good offer," McGeary countered. "It's only what you *can* offer."

Lucien untied his kerchief from his neck, and he used it to dab the beads of sweet clinging to his forehead. "No reason to get upset. I know you lost your boy. That's got to hurt. But it wasn't me who kilt him."

"Maybe not by your hand, but by your doin'."

"What are you sayin'? That I'm responsible fer what happened?"

"I'm sayin' Magnolia is for sale for four-hundred-thousand. I built it up from the dust, and I'd be a fool to sell for less."

The island woman, Cassandra, appeared with a pitcher of lemonade and a pair of tumblers. You all care for a nice drink?" she asked. "Made it fresh—water's cool from the well—best drink now before gets warm."

Lucien mumbled something indistinct, then taking a long drink of lemonade, he stepped off the porch. Taking the reigns of his stallion, he mounted the animal and blazed off, trailing a cloud of dust.

Cassandra watched as Lucien disappeared beyond the haze. "I puts a spell on him if you like," she said. "Man like him take a spell real good."

"Leave him be," McGeary instructed. "Man like him destroys hisself. Don't need nobody's help."

"Maybe you's right," said Cassandra, lifting the tumbler Lucien drank from. She held it beneath her nose and smelled its rim.

"A little potion, though, helps things along." She wiped the tumbler clean with her apron. "He's an evil man. Maybe's got a spell on hisself already." Cassandra was alone now, for McGeary had slipped into the house. "Yeah, he got a spell on hisself already," she said once more. "Yeah, he do."

As the days passed, Lucien began upping his offer, going all the way to three-hundred-thousand dollars. When McGeary refused to budge off his number, Lucien began to ache so badly for Magnolia that he sought the participation of investors.

It was a slow, cigar afternoon when the investors got together with Lucien. Magnolia trees were in bloom, and Mother Nature decorated the exterior of Lucien's home with large, white blossoms. Lucien's house was by far the most opulent in the county. It had taken ten convicts four months to build it. Constructed of pine, pecan, and oak, it had over five-thousand square feet of floor space, six bedrooms, two stairways and an enormous dining room. It also had a library, which Lucien cared little for, but it impressed the bankers he did business with.

"How much you figure McGeary's place is worth?" asked Sol Fleshman, a well-dressed businessman who was born and bred in Chicago. Although he earned his fortune in the south, Sol rarely comported himself as a southern. However, sometimes he'd turn a southern phrase. "I'm talking cash on the barrelhead," he said, laggardly pacing the porch, his hands behind his back.

"It ain't so much what it's worth today," said Lucien. "But what it's gonna be worth in the future. It's the future we're buying into. McGeary's got the biggest mill in the county, and a town's grown up on his land."

Clinton Madison, a straight-talking attorney from the state capitol, rubbed his chin with the back of his hand. "It's not much of a town," he expressed. "More a village than anything else. It has nothing but dirt roads and shanties. For God's sake, the town doesn't even have a name."

"Sugar Town might be a good name for it," said Lucien.

Sol Fleshman laughed. "Sounds like a damned red-light district!"

Clinton Madison did not share his associate's mirth. "What else can you tell us about McGeary's place?" he asked corporately.

"McGeary built a private rail," Lucien replied. "One day the Midwest Southern Railroad will connect with it. You gentlemen know what that means. I don't have the education you got, but I know things you folks don't. I know the land, and I tell you this, Sugar Town or whatever-the-hell you wanna call it, is gonna be the main junction between the coast and the capital. There's big money to be made in sugar these days, and we'll have leasing rights to hundreds of convicts."

Sol inserted a cigar into the corner of his mouth. "A rail, well, that is something," he said. "But four-hundred-thousand dollars is a lot of money."

"I'll come up with half," Lucien offered. "You fellas come up with the rest. I'll manage our interests and report on our profits every ninety days. You'll be welcome to visit at any time. Build a home here if you like. Timber is plentiful north of here, and convict labor costs almost nothing. Hell, build a mansion if you want."

"In this mosquito-infested river bed?" Sol asked incredulously.

"You'll find the county grows on ya," said Lucien. "Especially when you're countin' the money it makes." He broke the seal on a bottle of whiskey, and setting it on the table, he waited for someone to reach for a drink.

It was Sol Fleshman. "If I build a house it'll be miles away from the smoke of those damn mills," he said. "Besides, I don't care to live in a town of ex-convicts."

"Ex-convicts are the best kind of field hands," Lucien explained. "They knows where they been, and they don't wanna go back."

Clinton Madison listened lawyer-like. When a lull occurred in the conversation, he laid down the law. "We'll have no public killing of Negroes—convict or free man," he said. "South Fort County may be the frontier, but it must be lawful."

"If it's got to be done, then it needs to be quiet," Sol Fleshman added.

Lucien smoldered with the idea that his new partners were already giving him orders. He reached for the bottle, and pouring himself a drink, he took a gulp.

"You fellas are gonna be rich," Lucien promised.

"We're already rich," Clinton replied. "We simply want more money, and we want it without problems."

"There'll be no problems," Lucien said. "No problems at all."

The next day, Lucien hustled over to McGeary's place and announced the news. "The deal is done like you wanted," he began. "Four-hundred thousand in cash. We can finish things up within thirty days. Clinton Madison is an attorney from the capital. He's a partner and he'll handle the paperwork." McGeary sat calmly and politely listened to Lucien. "You'll be happy to get out of this place," Lucien continued. "Enjoy the California weather. I hope bygones will be bygones. No reason why we can't be friends."

"Well, ole' friend," McGeary began cynically. "Sorry to put you to such trouble, but I heard from the Midwest Southern Railroad yesterday. They wanna connect with my private rail as soon as possible. They'll begin freight service in and out of town. It'll be great for the cane business. I'd be a fool to sell now with the town growin' an' all."

Lucien's blood pressure shot up, and his face grew red with anger. McGeary read the rage in Lucien's countenance. "There's more opportunity to buy land," said McGeary, trying to sooth Lucien's agitation. "The Marin tract to the north is 33,000 acres of piney wood. The Jacinto tract to the east is 45,000 acres of wet land. You might could buy any one of them for 60,000 dollars. There's a big future out here, and plenty opportunity for everybody."

Lucien was infuriated. "I don't want no damn Marin tract or no Jacinto tract," he retorted. "You agreed to sell Magnolia, and now you back out of the deal. I always figured you for a coward, but not for a liar and a cheat. You'll regret what you done. I'll see to that." Lucien mounted his stallion, but before riding off, he gazed at McGeary menacingly. "You mark my words. I'll see you pay for this."

McGeary did not react, except to grin and to slide into a rocker. However, in the days ahead, he began to wear a Colt revolver on his hip and a small pistol inside his vest. He also kept a shotgun in his wagon, and whenever he was out alone, he kept the weapon close at hand.

10.

When Beatrice Baudelaire learned that Captain McGeary intended to remain at Magnolia, she was at first surprised, then she became angry. "Addison, I thought we had an agreement," she said in a controlled, but strained tone of voice. "I understood we would go to California—that you would sell Magnolia."

McGeary crouched down, and he examined a convict's repair work on a wagon wheel. "Things change out here," he told Beatrice without looking up at her.

Annoyed by his comment, she languished in her dilemma. A mosquito buzzed her skin, and she brushed it away. "You don't expect me to live in this—this—hell hole, do you?"

McGeary stood. Seeing Beatrice on the verge of tears, he knew she would soon sob without restraint. He lifted her chin, and he brought her eyes to meet his. "I got word from the railroad," McGeary began. "We'll have freight service to Magnolia within sixty days. The next step is passenger service. Magnolia will grow into a big town in the years to come. We'll be the main junction between the coast and the capitol. Within a decade, Magnolia will be worth millions."

"A decade?" Beatrice cried. "You don't expect me to live here for ten years, do you?"

McGeary thought about it. "I guess not," he confessed.

"What do I do now?" Beatrice asked. "I left the coast with everything I own. I've no place to go and little cash to leave with. But I can't stay here much longer, Addison. It's absolutely unbearable in this place. I'm afraid that—" she hesitated, then continued on, tears cascading down her cheeks. "I'll have to work once more in a brothel."

Covering her face with her hands, she cried like a child and fled from McGeary. He chased after her, and he found her inside a nearby warehouse. Beatrice often came to the warehouse during the afternoon hours when the heat was most stifling, where she could nest in the cool air.

"I know I made promises," McGeary said. "It's only right I help you get started in business somewhere." A guilty conscience weighed down on him. Beatrice held a special place in his heart. All her life men had wronged her, and her father provided the greatest injustice. He married her off by arrangement to a man in America, shipping her away on a rickety sea vessel. When the boat finally limped into the Caribbean, it was taking on water. Beatrice was relieved to arrive in New Orleans, but after a month with her new husband, she realized she exchanged a watery hell for a fiery one. Her husband owned a brothel, and he made his new wife the center-piece of his merchandise. One day the husband disappeared, and Beatrice traveled west, eventually ending up in Coastal City. "I imagine you could operate a boarding house," McGeary added. "Or a small hotel; maybe even a saloon."

The proposition delighted Beatrice. "Oh, darling," she sighed. "That would be wonderful."

"How much cash you figure you need to get set up in California?" McGeary asked. He had a figure in mind, but he wanted to know what Beatrice thought.

She was undecided about money. "I don't know," she replied. "Where should I go in California? I've heard it's nice in Sacramento."

"It's a pretty place," McGeary agreed. "And growing by leaps and bounds."

"Then I'll go to Sacramento," Beatrice affirmed. She embraced McGeary and sighed sensuously. "How much cash do *you* think I'll need?"

"I've got twenty-five thousand in cash put away for a rainy day."

"Twenty-five thousand! Addison, that's sooo generous."

"Consider it a business proposal. We'll be partners. I'll give you five-thousand dollars now. When you find a good opportunity in Sacramento, send me a telegraph, and I'll wire twenty-thousand to your bank."

"Addison, I knew I could count on you."

"Take whatever you need from the house. I imagine Cassandra will go with you."

Beatrice thought for a moment. "No, I think it's best that she stays."

McGeary grinned. "Well, I imagine I can use a magic potion at times." He laughed heartily, but Beatrice wasn't entertained by his remark.

"You shouldn't laugh, Addison," she warned. "Cassandra is an island woman, a descendant of people who practice witchcraft. She's a woman of power and magic." Beatrice sighed gently. The hot, heavy air had lifted, and a light breeze ushered in, allowing her to breathe effortlessly. "You might never learn what Cassandra does," she added. "Witches keep things secret. But no harm will come to you while she's here."

"If she's so valuable, then why give her to me?" McGeary asked. "Why not take her to California?"

"Because I want her to keep you safe," Beatrice replied. "You need someone to protect you."

11.

Beatrice's final days at Magnolia were uneventful, except when she and McGeary encountered Lucien at the rail station. Mr. Browski, a traveling hardware salesman, had set up his wagon, and McGeary was interested in a Winchester that Browski had for sale. Beatrice went along with him, accompanied by Silas, an outsized, muscular black man who did the heavy chores in McGeary's household. Silas and Beatrice poked around the rear-gate of Browski's wagon, admiring sundry items while McGeary waited for Browski to appear. It wasn't long before a section of the wagon's canvas went up, and Browski tipped his hat to welcome his customers.

"Where's the Winchester?" McGeary asked, ignoring all formalities.

"Just sold it," Browski replied. "To Mr. Eliot."

"When you gonna get another in?" McGeary quizzed.

"Probably not 'til winter," replied Browski. He dusted off a top-hat with a few swipes of a rag. "The gun's on back order," he explained, hanging up the hat for all to see. "It's selling everywhere like hotcakes."

Lucien appeared out of nowhere. "Yep, it's a mighty fine weapon," he said, proffering his opinion. "The first Winchester to use the new smokeless gunpowder. A rifleman in the hills can drop a man from 300 yards out. The best part is, nobody can figure where the shot came from. No gun smoke, no sign of the shooter."

Lucien words produced hostility between the landowners, and Beatrice stepped between them. "Addison, we should be going now," she said.

"You go along," McGeary told her. "I'll be home shortly." Beatrice gave him a pleading look, but she was unsuccessful in reversing his decision. "Silas, see Miss Beatrice gets back all right," he instructed.

Silas was an obedient man, but he was also gallant and a loyal employee. "No, Captain," he replied. "I gots to stay."

Beatrice admired Silas for his devotion, and she appreciated him for wanting to remain with McGeary. "I'll be fine, Addison," she said, opening a dainty umbrella to the sun. Then, lifting the hem of her dress a few inches, she scooted over ground toward home.

Once Beatrice was out of sight, McGeary spoke to Lucien fearlessly. "When I was an officer for the Confederacy, you was a kid still suckin' on a sugar rag." Silas didn't know whether to laugh or cry, for it was uncertain who would draw a weapon. "It seems to me you're too young to handle a gun," McGeary continued. "Maybe I should take it from you and give you a good spankin'." Hearing this, Silas became so upset, he nearly wet his pants. McGeary, though, kept his nerve, and waited for Lucien to make a move.

Lucien stepped back and lowered his rifle in the direction of McGeary.

Browski, though, had ideas of his own. "You fellas settle down," he said, brandishing a loaded shotgun. "The first man to move his weapon will have my lead to deal with." Browski was not a violent man, but he had the stomach to fire. "It's been twenty years since I killed a man," he explained. "I reckon I'm ready for another."

McGeary accepted Browski's words unequivocally, and when the pressure of the situation abated, he brushed past Lucien and walked off. Silas ran to catch up to the captain, continuously peering back over his shoulder, looking to see what Lucien might do. Lucien did nothing, but merely watched as McGeary strolled away.

12.

When Beatrice departed Magnolia, harvest season had just begun. Flames from burning furrows of cane chased reptiles out of their hovels, making it safe for convicts to enter the fields without fear of vermin and poisonous snakes. Leaves of cane fell in ashes along the furrows, laying scorched and flickering in the fire's aftermath. Leaving town in her carriage, Beatrice realized she would likely not return. She would forget the smell of smoke, the God-awful heat, and too the insects that feasted on human blood. She would forget the seemingly endless miles of fields, and the hot, stale air. She looked back at Magnolia one last time. The old plantation, now at a distance, appeared surprisingly luxurious. Silver smoke flowed above the town, floating languidly beneath a section of blue sky. The sky was alive with a fiery-red sun, and it intensely broke through layers of smoke to illuminate the landscape below. Wagons laden with cane trekked out of the fields toward town, and machetes wielded by black men glimmered. Beatrice turned her eyes away, and a final image of Magnolia lingered in her mind. She wondered why she hadn't seen Magnolia's splendor before; why she had never perceived that the land of cane is heavenly and abundant.

13.

Late in the year 1879 McGeary began to think about getting a wife. He was not alone in Magnolia, for he had the island woman who managed his household, and too the black women who cooked and helped with chores. But he wanted a companion, a woman to keep him from feeling alone, perhaps one he could love. McGeary had sugar customers in Red Valley, an isolated strip of fertile land two days ride by train and wagon. He figured it was a good place to find a wife, and he promised himself to keep an eye out for prospects on his next visit.

McGeary realized that the wife he selected couldn't be just any woman, for she would be a frontier wife. She couldn't be endeared to parties or other gaieties of life, but rather she would have to endure the invasions of mosquitoes, the overwhelming heat of summer, and the dense humidity of the rainy season.

McGeary left for Red River in late September. The stifling heat had abated, and a northwest wind swept into Magnolia, making the sky enormously blue and bright. Field hands gleefully cut cane, relishing in the cool, unsullied air. It was a rare day when one could see beyond the mills and glimpse the banks of the river; and then in the evening when darkness descends watch the stars glimmer on the velvet of black sky.

Arriving to Red Valley, a young woman immediately caught McGeary's fancy. She was a mixed-blood Indian, some Spanish, or perhaps French. The girl had recently arrived to the area with her parents, indigenous farmers coming off a bad season. The father, a slender but muscular man, was looking for any kind of work to feed his family. However, he had found nothing, and he likely wouldn't until early spring. McGeary watched the girl each day from afar, admiring her features from the corner of his eye. She was a tall, bronze-skin woman. Her black hair was cropped amateurishly, but she wore it shoulder-length, causing it to hang down in natural waves, like that of affluent white girls.

Having considered his options, McGeary approached a *Tejano* who spoke the girl's language.

McGeary frankly addressed the man. "You think the girl's folks will object to marriage?" he asked. "Perhaps I should offer them some gold."

The Tejano tipped back his *vaquero* hat, and it exposed his forehead. "She's not for sale," he replied indignantly.

"I'm sorry if I offended you," McGeary apologized.

The Tejano picked on a splinter of wood on the wall of a dry goods store. "It's not like it used to be," he commented. "Not like the old days of buying and selling Negroes. If the girl wants to marry, then it's her decision. Magdalena's her name. If she likes you, she'll go with you. She's a young woman, and she can do as she pleases."

McGeary asked for clarification. "You sayin' it's possible for me to have the girl?" he asked.

The Tejano winked at McGeary. "Sure," he said, barely above a whisper. "The girl has her eye on you too. Buy a gift for the girl's mother and father. I'll put in a few good words for you." He paused a moment, then added, "five-hundred-dollars cash will be due for my services."

"If I'm able to take the girl," said McGeary. "You'll have the five-hundred." The captain was content with the figure, for he thought he'd have to pay much more. His eyes gravitated to the girl who stood nearby on the sidewalk, observing the world with innocent, vivacious eyes.

"I'll do as you say," McGeary informed the Tejano. "I plan on leavin' in a couple days, and I'd like take the girl with me."

The Tejano nodded in agreement. "Stop by the hotel this evening," he said. "I'll introduce you. You can buy dinner for the family. I'm sure it'll help the father sleep well tonight."

"Where's the family stayin'?" asked McGeary.

"Outside town," the Tejano answered. "Along the river. Most folks stay out there—poor folks, anyway"

McGeary drew a gold coin from his pocket. "They might wanna stay at the hotel tonight," he suggested. "It pains me to think the girl's got to sleep on the ground."

After sunset, McGeary went to the hotel, and he found Magdalena and her family propped at a dinner table. The parent's faces mirrored the life of aging peasants, but Magdalena's appearance spoke of youthful womanhood. McGeary found her intriguing, but standing before the family, he was at a loss for words to express his feelings. Somehow, however, he managed to amicably utter, "what's for dinner?"

Magdalena spoke with a jumbled cadence. "I think roast—pot-roast," she replied. "What is—pot-roast?"

McGeary was about to laugh, but the door to the dining room opened, and the Tejano stepped through, the atmosphere altering upon his abrupt appearance.

"My, oh my," said the Tejano. "That's a nice picture of a family. Yeah, a real nice picture."

McGeary recognized a tone of derisiveness in his voice. He stepped away from the table and approached the Tejano. "What's goin' on?" he asked

The Tejano was quick to reply. "I thought you'd like to get to know everyone."

McGeary surveyed the table, and saw four members of the family. A young boy about four years of age sat next to Magdalena, and the mother and father sat across from them.

"There was one more," the Tejano said. "A child about two years old. He died of fever during their journey."

"How many know English?"

"Only the girl. But not much."

"I brought a gift for her folks—a knife for her pa, and a mirror for her ma. I got a dress for the girl, but she needs to be fitted for it."

The Tejano translated the information to the girl's folks. The father nodded agreeably and the mother smiled. A door to the kitchen burst open, and the proprietor of the hotel delivered dinner to the table. Magdalena's father was not bashful, but heaped meat and potatoes on his plate.

"I'm sure they'll be happy with you," the Tejano assured McGeary. "The old man has a few good years of work left in him, and the mother claims to be a good cook."

"What in hell's name are you sayin'?" McGeary asked.

"The girl wants to leave with you," the Tejano explained. "But she'll go nowhere without her little brother. The problem is the girl's folks won't give up the boy. So, the way I see it, you take everyone, or you take nobody."

McGeary abhorred the idea. "I'll be hog-tied," he said.

"Look at it this way," the Tejano suggested. "You're getting four for the price of one."

McGeary peered at the Tejano like a hanging judge. "I need to sleep on it," he stated. Twisting the frame of his body, McGeary moved to leave. However, he stopped, and looking back at Magdalena, his eyes engaged hers. Her face brightened, and the sight of her smile compelled McGeary's spirit to soar. "Have them ready tomorrow at dawn," he told the Tejano. "I'll be leavin' earlier than expected."

14.

The distance between McGeary's home and the rail station was nearly a mile. Nevertheless, when McGeary stepped off the train, word of his arrival had already reached his household, and Cassandra waited on the porch to welcome him.

"Good to see ya, Captain," she said. "If you like, I'll draw ya a bath. Bedroom's clean, and the linens been washed." She peered beyond McGeary, and she saw the family. "We got guests, Captain?"

"Oh, well, yeah," McGeary mumbled, attempting to gather his thoughts. He stepped down, and he gestured bashfully. "This is Magdalena. And this is her family."

Wheels spun caustically in Cassandra's mind. "Hummm, I see," she said. "I guess I'll have 'em shown a room." Her mind's rotations slowed, and she shouted into the house. "Miz Bessie, come on out here!"

Bessie James came through the door wearing a kitchen apron. A robust black woman, she was respected by everyone, for she was humble and God-fearing. When the judge gave her husband "Crazy Wilkie" three years in prison, Bessie left her home in Mobile and traveled all the way to Magnolia to be near him. Each night she slept outdoors, earning a few pennies here and there by sewing and cooking. McGeary heard about Bessie and figured to give her the use of a shanty, but after meeting her, he saw something that he had never seen before in a women or a man. It was an inner brightness, a light that gave evidence of her faith and will. McGeary invited Bessie to work in his household. She accepted and negotiated a salary for herself of two dollars a week with meals and board.

"Show these folks the guest room," Cassandra said. Bessie nodded respectfully, and she led the family away. "I 'magine the girl should stay in your room," Cassandra said to McGeary.

The captain stood beside his wagon, his head tilted onto the cup of his hand. "Maybe," he said vaguely. "And maybe not."

Following a prolonged silence, Cassandra made an admission. "I'm sorry, Captain," she disclosed. "I didn't know that potion was gonna be so mighty."

"What are you talkin' about?" McGeary asked.

"Well, I knowed you was lookin' for a wife," she began. "I figured to help things along. I didn't make a potion for gettin' a whole family, though. Things just turned out that way."

McGeary didn't scold Cassandra, but rather he coached her fatherly. "They'll be no more making of potions," he firmly said. "At least not without talkin' to me."

"Yes sir, Captain," Cassandra responded. "I can do that."

15.

Everyone was exhausted from their journey and headed for bed early. Bessie gave the large, extra bedroom to the family. It was nicely furnished with a pair of oak beds, an armoire, and a cedar chest that had a sweet, woodsy scent. The family found the room to their liking, in particular, the mother, who shuttled about putting clothes and trinkets in proper places while her husband slipped into bed and relaxed. Magdalena, after a hot bath, put on a night gown, and finding a comfortable chair in the bedroom, she sat down. Her father lifted up his head and stared curiously at his daughter. He grunted a few words and Magdalena reacted by turning her attention to her mother who, apparently agreeing with her husband, shooed her daughter out of the room.

McGeary slept lightly that evening, which is unusual for him, but he had been thinking about Magdalena while lying in bed, his mind alert with sensual images. His bedroom door squeaked open, causing him to become animated and to rub his eyes. Focusing his sight, he saw Magdalena standing in the doorway, appearing peaceful and lovely. She ran her fingers through her hair, helping its strands flow down upon her shoulders. A lamp in the hallway shone through her nightdress, allowing McGeary to see the curve of her hips and the shape of her legs. She allowed the straps of her nightdress to fall, exposing her small, innocent breasts. McGeary sat up in bed, and Magdalena crossed over to him. He patted the bed, indicating that she should sit.

"You're prettier than I figured," he said.

"No man before," she mumbled in response.

McGeary could only guess what Magdalena wished to express. "I'm the first?" he asked.

"Yes," she replied.

McGeary smiled. "We can take our time," he began. "We'll travel to the coast in a few days. Have some time alone. See a preacher about getting wedding papers." He was not sure Magdalena understood. "You understand?" he asked.

She grinned, indicating that she did.

The next morning was hazily humid. Cassandra awakened early, and she went into the kitchen to begin preparing a lavish meal for McGeary's newly-acquired family. Ordinarily, Bessie arose at dawn, arriving to the kitchen before everyone else. But on this particular morning, she was absent, and Cassandra, concerned for Bessie, went outdoors to find her.

Cassandra found Bessie beneath a tree behind the house, which is where Bessie always came whenever she felt discouraged. She sat in a wobbly chair, her head bowed, and her eyes shut to reality.

"What's botherin' you, Miz Bessie?" asked Cassandra.

"I come all the way from Mobile to be near my husband," she replied. "It been a whole year now, and I ain't seen Wilkie but one day."

"Why not?" asked Cassandra. "He's inside the prison, and you can visit him, can't you?"

"Yeah," replied Bessie. "But he be *down-low* going on six months." Down-low was a hovel dug out of the ground where the most incorrigible convicts were sent for isolated confinement. "They say down-low's no place for man or beast, and I worries 'bout him."

"Best you talk to the captain," said Cassandra. "He know 'bout such things."

"I don't likes askin' folks for nothin'," said Bessie. "I guess, though, sometimes ain't no other way."

As soon as the opportunity presented itself, Cassandra told McGeary about Bessie. "She be needing help, Captain," Cassandra said. "But Bessie ain't the kind to ask folks for things."

"What does she need?" asked McGeary.

"Best she tell you herself," replied Cassandra. "She out back in her place under the tree."

McGeary headed outdoors, and when Bessie saw him come toward her, she got out of her chair, greeting him face to face. "Morning, Captain," she said meekly.

McGeary placed his hand on Bessie's shoulder. "What can I do to help, Bessie?" he asked. "Don't you know to come to me if you need somethin'?"

"It be my husband, Wilkie," she replied. "They got him down-low and ain't nobody can see him. I worries, Captain. I worries all the time."

"Don't worry anymore," he said. "Tomorrow I'll go to the prison and see what I can do."

16.

Armed sentries atop the prison wall recognized McGeary as he approached, and they shouted to the guards below to open the timber-hewn gate. McGeary entered and was met by the Lieutenant of the Guards.

"You come to see the warden?" asked the lieutenant.

"I imagine so," McGeary replied. "But I first wants to see the convict Wilkie James."

"Wilkie?" asked the lieutenant. "Crazy Wilkie?"

"That's right," McGeary replied. "Wilkie James."

"Crazy Wilkie's down-low," the lieutenant said. "You don't want to go there."

"Maybe not," said McGeary. "All the same, though, I want to see Wilkie."

"You'll have to talk to the warden," the lieutenant explained. "No free man's ever gone down-low, except for me and the guards."

The warden's office was on the upper floor of the central building of the prison, and it allowed him to look out his window into the yard below. At the end of each day, he watched the tired gangs of shackled convicts trudge in from the fields in double-file, and later he observed them as they served themselves from rows of iron kettles filled with beans, okra and rice. Once a week

51

the landowners who held leases on the convicts fed them meat, cornbread, and small squares of cake, which they devoured with such delight that the guards would become envious and invite themselves to eat. In the cane fields, it was something entirely different. At noon, the convicts ate day-old prison bread and whatever morsels they had managed to squirrel away from prior meals. By far, the tastiest and most revitalizing part of the meal was the fresh barrels of water that were freighted into the fields by wagon. They drank the clear, cool liquid ceremoniously, savoring each sip as if it was the water from the last spring of the earth.

When McGeary entered the warden's office, he found the prison boss at his perch by the window peering out into an empty prison yard. "I saw you come in the gate," he said without turning around to welcome McGeary. "But I didn't see that crate of whiskey you always bring me."

"I've got somethin' better than whiskey," said McGeary. He reached inside his shirt and drew out his lease payment. "There's a little somethin' extra in it for you."

The warden turned to face McGeary, a crooked smile on his face. A wide-bellied man of peculiar graces, he wore his thinning hair lacquered back over his ears. His paunchy waist was bound by a thick, leather belt that was carved with a series of five-pointed stars. The belt was more decorative than functional, for his trousers were actually held up by pair of suspenders, which the warden's thumbs habitually toyed with. Whenever the warden became annoyed, he would bind up the straps of his suspenders so tightly that his trousers rose up to reveal his snakeskin boots.

"Thanks, Captain," said the warden, accepting the cash. "By the time I pass this out to every politician in the state, there's not much left for me." He placed the money in a drawer of his desk, and he locked the drawer with a key. "So, tell me, Captain, what makes me deserving of such generosity?" The warden slipped the key into his vest pocket. Lifting a nail file from his desk, he began to reshape the nail of his index finger. "I've been around long enough to know that something always requires something in return."

"I wanna put Wilkie James out on lease," McGeary responded. "His wife, Bessie, works for me. She ain't seen him in months, and she worries about him."

"Yeah, I'd worry, too, if I was her," said the warden. "Most convicts down-low only come up when they're dead." McGeary did not comment, only gazed vacantly at the warden. "These things require hard, cold cash," the warden continued. "It's how things are done." He studied his nails, scrutinizing them for specks of dirt. "Our business in South Fort County isn't going to last forever. I hear that the Federals don't much like the idea of leasing convicts."

"Why's that?" McGeary asked.

"Nobody knows exactly politicians think," replied the warden. "Maybe it's got something to do with slavery, or maybe they just don't like the way the South does business." Then almost as an afterthought, the warden asked, "how much extra is there in this month's lease payment?"

"Five-hundred dollars," McGeary replied.

"Make it a thousand," said the warden. "And I'm sure I can accommodate you on the Wilkie James situation. Keep in mind, though, he'll now be your responsibility."

An hour later, McGeary departed the prison with Wilkie James, and the two men rode together toward town. They arrived to the stable next to the train depot, and here McGeary split Wilkie's chains with an axe.

"My place is a mile down the road," McGeary informed Wilkie. "Bessie's there waitin'. I got work to do here."

Wilkie journeyed down the road, not bothering to utter a word of thanks to McGeary. He stayed with Bessie that evening in her small quarters next to the kitchen. In the morning, Silas re-shackled Wilkie, and he took him by wagon out to the fields where a gang of convicts harvested cane with machetes. At the end of the day, Wilkie returned to the prison, but now he slept in the barracks with the other convicts.

17.

Two weeks after Magdalena arrived in Magnolia, she and McGeary boarded a train for the coast. They arrived mid-afternoon and hired a carriage to cruise the shoreline. They passed along golden dunes and foaming beaches, the salty air sharpening their awareness of the world around them. Meandering back through town, the carriage passed an enclosed area where men and women laughed boisterously in the street. The partiers danced drunkenly, flailing to the music of guitarists while armed police patrolled outside the gate.

"What is?" Magdalena asked in broken English.

"The Open District," McGeary replied. "A haven for the world's fugitives and thieves. All kinds of sinful men are there, some who'll murder as easy as they breathe."

Unable to comprehend, Magdalena ceased looking at the Open District. McGeary cracked his carriage whip, and the horses were obliged to trot. Within minutes, the couple arrived to a sawdust-floor restaurant and took a table at a bay-front window. Feasting on crab cakes and flounder, they watched small vessels sail in from the ocean. The boats navigated the bay easily despite stout winds whipping up froth on the surface of the water.

McGeary looked at this pocket watch and saw that it was six o'clock. He walked Magdalena back to the hotel and told her to rest for awhile. The old gambler had been itching to play poker for weeks, and strolling to a nearby saloon, he slid into a low-stakes table.

Two hours later, McGeary was down two-hundred dollars. However, it mattered little to him, for he played to enjoy the game and not to win. This day, Magdalena was foremost on his mind.

"Ain't like you, Captain," said a starched-shirt gentleman at the poker table. "You got a run of bad luck."

"Well, it don't bother me none," responded McGeary. "I hope you fellas can put my money to some use."

"Hell, yeah, we can put it to use!" exclaimed another man. "Bartender! Another bottle of bourbon!"

Everyone at the table laughed, and when the bottle arrived, they drank heartily. McGeary wiped his lips dry on his sleeve and began to deal. "A couple more hands, boys," he announced. "Then I gotta get back to the hotel."

An hour later, McGeary stepped out into the night. The wind that gusted earlier in the day had risen, and small branches of trees tumbled in the streets. Rain fell in squalls, spinning with the wind and draining along street gutters. Unconcerned with the storm, McGeary turned up the collar of his jacket and charged headlong into the rain.

Arriving to the hotel, McGeary noticed that its windows were shuttered. At the front desk, a bleary-eyed clerk counted money from a cash drawer. Looking up, he saw the captain enter the lobby.

"No need to worry, Captain," the desk clerk said, placing a mound of cash into the hotel's safe. "Coastal City has storms all the time. I remember the storm of 1868. Some say it was a hurricane, but I don't think so. Many folks died, though."

"How many were lost in the storm?" McGeary asked.

"Oh, twenty or thirty as I recall," the clerk answered.

McGeary departed the lobby, and he ascended the stairs to his room where Magdalena was sleeping soundly. McGeary leaned over her, and with a trembling hand, he pressed a finger lightly to her lips. Not having the heart to wake her, he stretched out on a sofa, and within moments he was asleep.

McGeary was roused from sleep at midnight by the blare of a train whistle. Curious about the sound, he left the room and went downstairs only to find the lobby empty. He yanked open the entrance door of the hotel, and a hard wind blew in, ruffling the curtains hanging on the windows and walls. Looking out into the blustering night, his instincts told him the storm was rising. He walked the short distance to the train station, and he was astonished to see that a crowd had gathered on the platform. He pushed through the mass, and he got the attention of the boarding agent.

"What's going on?" McGeary asked.

"Train's going out," the agent replied.

"It's not due to leave 'til morning," said McGeary.

"Can't wait," the agent responded. "Water's already over the tracks on the north side of town. Another hour and the tracks will be impassable."

McGeary reached into his pocket for cash. "I'll take two tickets," he declared.

"Train's full," the agent revealed. "Not even standing room's available."

"Then how in hell's name do we get out of here?" he asked, perturbed with the railroad employee.

"Get yourself a boat," the agent suggested glibly. He tried to turn away, but the captain turned him back by a jerk of his shoulder.

"A pair of tickets are six dollars," McGeary said. "Here's two-hundred and six."

The agent admired the cash, and quickly snatched the bills from McGeary's hand. "Take a seat there," he said, pointing to an empty coach-car three-hundred feet down the track. "The train departs once it hooks the car. That should be in about twenty minutes."

"I'll be back," McGeary announced.

"Make sure you are," the agent warned. "The train waits for nobody."

His boots heavily soaked, McGeary sloshed back to the hotel. Entering his room, he urgently awakened Magdalena. "Get dressed," he told her. "We're leaving out."

Magdalena rubbed her eyes, unwilling to awaken. However, she obeyed her husband. Not bothering to ask for an explanation, she quickly dressed and began to pack.

"No time for that," said McGeary.

The couple left their luggage behind and hurried off downstairs. Going out into the driving rain, they negotiated their way around rising water. The flooding made McGeary apprehensive, but he masked his fear for the sake of Magdalena who was terrified by the storm..

When they arrived to the station, the engine was already moving back down the track, sluggishly churning in reverse. It bumped the empty coach-car with a clang, and then it immediately crooned forward. McGeary did not wait for the train to reach the platform, but rather he marched down the track and hopped aboard. As the engine rolled in, he grasped Magdalena's hands and lifted her out of the crowd, allowing her to step onto the train. Acquiring seats by a window, the couple looked out at the burgeoning crowd. The mob was close to panic, and the agent worked to control it. He was only mildly successful, for the crowd pushed forward and anxiously spilled over, filling the car within minutes. The agent didn't bother to ask for tickets, but he simply motioned to the engineer to roll. The engine steamed forward despite the men and women who clung to the exterior of the train. Some people fell away while others reached the train's roof; lying low and holding tightly, they braced for the ride of their lives.

18.

It was after midnight, but outside his window, McGeary could see the undersides of clouds glowing with energy. He observed the stormy world, watching waters rapidly flow, rising and threatening the life of Coastal City. McGeary knew that people would die that night, and the thought of death distressed him. It reminded him of the war, and many destroyed by clashing of armies. He tried not to think of death, but he couldn't discharge the memory of war from his mind. He wondered whether the drowned soul was as ugly as the burned soul, if death by water was equal to death by fire. He gazed at Magdalena and wished to speak, but he couldn't find the words to express his thoughts. She seemed to know what he was thinking, however, for she tightened her lips and forced a smile.

Levering himself out of his seat, McGeary stood upright. Unwilling to look Magdalena in the eye, he turned his face away and pushed off down the aisle. Sliding the rear door open, he saw an area of high ground and stepped off the train.

McGeary needed to garner supplies, and despite the raging weather, he explored through high water and found a hardware store. It was closed, of course, and also securely locked. But McGeary slammed his shoulder against the door, and it burst open, the big man lurching forward. Searching inside the store, he found something he needed. Suddenly, however, McGeary heard a voice behind him.

"Don't move," said the voice. "I've got a shotgun. I'll use it."

"Who are you?" McGeary asked. "What do you want?"

"Who am I?" the voice responded. "Who the hell are you?"

"Captain Addison McGeary."

"What are you doing breaking down doors, Captain?"

McGeary held up a heavy roll of hemp. "I figure this rope will help out in a flood."

"Yeah, it might in the right hands, of course."

"I can handle a rope," McGeary declared. "And I can handle a gun. I've handled a brigade of men, and I'd damn sure handle you if you didn't have a shotgun in your hand."

The man laughed. "I don't think that'd be a good idea," he said. "Beings I'm the sheriff."

McGeary was not in the mood for humor, and he refrained from warming up to the lawman.

When the sheriff's laughter subsided, he cleared his throat and spoke. "Take the rope, Captain," he said. "And take this, too." He tossed McGeary a metal badge. "You're now a deputy. The law's on your side."

McGeary placed the badge in his pocket without a display of satisfaction. The sheriff stepped forward judiciously, and he handed McGeary a slide-action pump shotgun. "You better take it," he said. "I'm sure there'll come a time to use it."

19.

McGeary did not journey far into the storm before he found a woman and her child clinging to the branches of a willow, flood waters rushing about them. He tossed the mother a line of rope, however, she was too frightened to take hold. Moments later, her hands slipped from the willow, and she and her child were swept away. McGeary could do nothing but watch as they disappeared beneath murky waves. He gathered up his rope, and he set it upon his shoulder. Again he journeyed onward, his large frame pushing through water like a mighty sea vessel. He arrived to a place not far from The Open District. The saloons and flop-houses inside the compound had already succumbed to the storm, and little remained except for the district's wrought-iron gate, which stood as a dismal reminder of the evil that once resided there.

A quarter-mile beyond the district was the shoreline, or what was once the shoreline, for between district and shore, every home was destroyed and no distinction between ocean and shore could be made. It seemed to McGeary strange, for the homes had been built on a mound of high-ground, and the flood waters there were drained and shallow. Then he spied something awesome, a huge wave rolling in from the ocean. Alarmed, McGeary backed up as far as he could and secured himself to the trunk of a tree. As the wave approached the shore, it was seven-feet high, or so McGeary calculated, and it rolled mightily onto the beach, sweeping away all obstacles and debris. As the tide drew back, objects began to bob in the water, and as they rose to the surface, McGeary saw that some were human bodies. An undertow earlier that day had sucked them into the ocean, and now the ocean had given them back. McGeary tried to shut his mind, but images of death continued to penetrate. The corpse of a woman floated by, her face and hands above water, her torso submerged below. McGeary lifted the woman's body to the water's surface and noticed she was well-dressed. An affluent lady, he guessed. She probably had lived in one of the seaside mansions. All well-constructed homes, she had likely figured that hers would withstand the wind, but she had not anticipated a lethal surge of water. McGeary took the dead woman by the hand and held it. How odd, he wondered, the body had a finger severed. He set his thoughts aside and released the woman, watching as she drifted back to the ocean, perhaps to reunite with loved ones, or simply to rest and to sleep.

Trudging onward again, he began to regret he had gotten off the train, to have traded a world of the living for a world of the dead. His mind turned through stages of worry. The dim, soaked sights of Coastal City seemed like purgatory, a location not of the earth, yet neither a heavenly place. He walked in hell, he considered, a valley of the shadow of death, a place for sobbing, a place for the gnashing of teeth.

McGeary saw human figures wading in the water, and focusing his eyes, he perceived they were men. He moved toward, and he closed in on one of the men, noticing his hand fishing about in the water. Appearing to grasp something, the man's face grew into a grin. Lifting a woman's hand out of the water, he drew a knife from his pants. He sliced her finger and pulled off a gold ring. The man washed the ring in the water, and then he dropped it into his pocket. Satisfied with himself, he smiled, exposing a mouth of rotted teeth. What transpired next in McGeary's soul only a God or Goddess may guess. For McGeary moved close to the man, and lifting his shotgun, he pointed it at his chest.

An explosion went off in the gun, and it blew the man three feet out of the water. McGeary plodded away, empty of all feelings, water spinning about him, like the wind out of Pandora's Box, turbulent, maligned, and fatal.

20.

At early dawn the storm began to calm, and slivers of sunshine broke through the clouds. Survivors roamed tearfully about in the mud searching for loved ones. Exhausted, McGeary did not attempt to assist them, but rather he cradled his shotgun in his arms and searched for higher ground. Somewhere along his journey, his legs became wobbly, and loosing consciousness, his body fell solidly to the ground.

An hour later, he was awakened by the heel of a boot jostling his ribs. His eyes opened and he saw the sheriff standing over him. "Thought maybe you was dead," the sheriff said. McGeary slowly rose up onto his feet, the sheriff studying him from head to toe. He was filthy, and blood dripped from the palms of his hands. His shirt was split at the seams as if it had been worn by a beast in a brawl. "Are you the fella that folks are talkin' about?" the sheriff asked.

"I don't know," replied McGeary. "Maybe so, maybe not."

"I guess it don't much matter," said the sheriff.

"Guess not," McGeary agreed. He then asked, "how many are dead?"

"Five-hundred, maybe more," the sheriff replied. He shook his head with remorse. "Work is just begun. I can use your help, Captain."

"I'm heading home," declared McGeary.

"Not for at least three days," said the sheriff. "The city's surrounded by miles of debris and flood water. It's impossible for a boat to get through. Train rails are being repaired, but it'll take time."

McGeary accepted his fate without complaint. "Any place where a man can eat?" he asked, his stomach growling. "How 'bout a beefsteak?"

"Hospital on the east side of town," the sheriff replied. "Come with me. I'm heading that way." The two men strolled off together. "Half the city's destroyed," the sheriff said as they walked. "It'll take years to rebuild. The folks that died, though, can't replace them. I was born here, and I got friends I'll miss." The sheriff paused for a moment, waiting for McGeary to share a sympathetic word with him. McGeary was impervious, though, and he had nothing to convey. "I'm responsible for the safety of Coastal City," the sheriff added. "I should've done more. Yeah, I should've done more."

The pair staggered along in concert, their shoulders drooped and their heads hung low. They came to a rise in the terrain and saw the hospital at its summit. Surrounded by a multitude of weary people, the edifice appeared to serve as a beacon for the living, and a headstone for the deceased.

McGeary's sense of smell told him that a meal was being served at the hospital's rear entrance. He trudged around back, and he saw an iron kettle cooking over a wood fire. A doctor in a white coat attended to it. "What do we got for a morning meal, Doc?" McGeary asked.

The doctor stirred the kettle. "Only this," he sullenly replied.

McGeary leaned over, and he peaked into the pot. "Looks like beans to me," he said.

The doctor preferred to not comment further, but McGeary's presence was compelling, and he thought to be polite. "Yeah, beans," he responded. "Cornbread's inside, baking in the oven."

"Eggs?" McGeary asked. "Where can I find them?"

"Eggs are for the sick," the doctor explained.

McGeary opened his lips to object, but he quickly pressed them back together. Summoning the nerve to say something, he finally uttered, "look, doctor—"

"I'm looking," the doctor sounded off. "And you don't look sick."

McGeary searched himself for a place to accommodate the doctor's words, but his hunger made the words unwelcome. He caught sight of a cow behind a shed, and it piqued his interest. "What about—" he began, but the doctor had played out the same conversation time and again with other men, and he smoothly repeated his stock response.

"It's for the sick."

McGeary knew that complaining was futile, for the doctor's interest was in nourishing the weak, and not in satiating the strong. Besides, he was becoming increasingly hungry, and the idea of beans and cornbread was beginning to sound appealing.

Four days passed before the train finally got through, reaching Coastal City in late-morning. Receiving word of the train's arrival, McGeary went immediately to the station, where, much to his surprise, he saw the sheriff waiting for him. "Thanks for everything, Captain," said the sheriff, extending his hand to McGeary. "I don't know what the town would have done without you."

McGeary shook the sheriff's hands like an old friend. "I didn't do too much," he said modestly.

"Whatever you say," responded the sheriff. He shuffled his foot, apparently searching for the proper words to speak. "About the deputy badge ….." he said at last.

McGeary removed the badge from his pocket, and he held it out for the sheriff to take.

"I don't want it back," the sheriff explained. "Keep it. You earned it."

McGeary wished to be courteous, but his words leapt out with force. "I can't stay in Coastal City, Sheriff," he said. "I gotta get home."

The sheriff was amused. "You're a strange fella," he said playfully. "I'm not asking you to stay."

McGeary didn't understand the reason for the sheriff's amusement. "What exactly *are* you asking?" he quizzed.

"Nothing," the sheriff replied. "You're an official Deputy Sheriff." The sheriff grinned amicably. "You'll find a badge comes in handy. Someday you might need it."

21.

Magdalena was at the Magnolia rail station when McGeary arrived. She had waited for him three days and slept on the ground each night, a light blanket covering her shoulders, and a pillow providing a soft place for her head. Her mother brought her food and begged her daughter to return to the house. Despite whatever her mother said, Magdalena stayed at the rail station and waited.

It was mid-afternoon when she heard the faint ring of a whistle. She didn't know if it was a train, for last night during her dreamy imaginings she had heard a similar sound. Now, however, she noticed a wisp of smoke in the distance, and its sight enlivened her with hope. The whistle sounded once more, and it gave her glee, causing her to bounce on the balls of her feet. At first sight of the train, she felt as if her spirit would burst, and she jiggled to and fro. The engine slowed and discharged steam, and McGeary appeared on the steps of a car. Magdalena rushed toward him, and the moment his feet touched the ground, she flung her arms about him.

"I'm okay," McGeary said in a mellow voice.

"You come back," she responded. "You come back."

"Yeah, I've come back," he affirmed. "Let's go home."

The couple walked together, Magdalena's arms circling McGeary's chest, her head resting upon his shoulder.

"I must look a mess," McGeary commented.

"Mess?" Magdalena asked, unfamiliar with the word.

"I know I look terrible," McGeary said, rephrasing his thought.

"Terrible, no," she responded. "Handsome, yes."

McGeary laughed heartily.

The captain's return to Magnolia surprised everyone in his household, except Cassandra who had been confident all along that he would come home safely. Most of the women could hardly speak, their voices shrilling as they hurried about the house, preparing for a celebratory dinner and heating large pots of water for the captain's bath.

He and Magdalena went up to their bedroom where she helped him out of his clothes. She brought him a robe, and pointing out a chair in which to sit, she used a boar-bristle brush to clean his hair. When the women were finished pouring warm water into a wide tub, Magdalena waved them off. McGeary dropped his robe, and he slipped into his bath, the fresh water relaxing his tired body. Magdalena applied a fine soap to his head, and she lovingly shampooed his hair. She washed his beard as well, cleaning and combing it with her delicate fingers. She disappeared for a moment and quickly returned with a surprise, which she held behind her back, shielding it from McGeary's eyes.

McGeary noticed. "What's ya got there?" he asked, recognizing a devilish look in her eyes.

Magdalena covered her mouth with her hand and softly laughed. Summoning the courage to show him, she produced a pair of cutting shears.

"What's ya gonna do with that," McGeary asked, drumming his fingers nervously on the tub's metal wall.

She snipped the air with her fingers, and it made a noise that mimicked the sound of cutting, "chp, chp."

"Oh, no, you don't," he responded.

"Little bit," she said. "Little bit."

McGeary thought about it. "Okay," he acquiesced. "But just a little."

"Yes, yes," she agreed.

Magdalena lifted the shears, and McGeary appeared to remain calm, but inside he was as jumpy as a caged wolf. Once Magdalena had removed an inch of his beard, she held a mirror up to his face, and he saw that it was fine work.

The bath now finished, Magdalena unfolded a few towels and set them flat on the bed. Signaling for her husband to lie down, she lifted a bottle of scented oil that had warmed on the sill of a window. She applied the oil to his flesh, and it made him groan with pleasure. Rubbing the oil in gently, she massaged his muscles, her hands constantly moving, touching even his soft places, causing him to drift into dreams. However, he would sleep only for a moment, for he would awaken to her hands, which thrilled his body and made him feel vital.

22.

Lucien Eliot couldn't disengage his mind from the fact that McGeary reneged on a deal and, moreover, he made him look like a fool with his business associates. Lucien nearly went mad with the idea, and with the humiliating episode rattling in his head, he began making murderous plans.

"I want the bastard killed," he announced one day while overseeing a convict gang working the cane fields. A hardened group of men, Lucien hoped that one would commit homicide. "Any man willin' to kill McGeary, I'll make rich." Lucien smirked and strutted with his hands on his hips. "How 'bout you?" he asked. "Or you, or you, or any man?"

"We's done with fightin, Mr. Lucien," a convict confessed. "Most us is short-time, and be goin' home."

"Why not go home rich?" Lucien asked.

"We be trusted," the convict replied. "If the warden know we talk 'bout killin', he gonna put us down-low. Ain't nobody wanna go down-low."

"Hell, the warden's my friend," Lucien boasted. "On my payroll too."

The convicts knew that it was best to ignore Lucien, and they set their attention on the cutting of cane.

Lucien kicked up dust in disgust. "Damn convict is as much a coward as McGeary," he cried.

A rider drew up on a painted stallion. Possessing a shotgun and a jellied stomach, he appeared to be the paradigm of a prison guard. His name was Thomas Brannon, but everyone called him "Ole Tom." A redneck known for his capable handling of prisoners, he supervised the work of one-hundred field hands.

"How 'bout you, Tom?" Lucien asked. "You wanna get rich?"

"I imagine ever'body wants to get rich."

"All you gots to do is kill McGeary."

Ole Tom laughed vigorously, his broad, taunt shoulders quaking. The shotgun, though, remained firmly on his hip. "You gots me wrong," he told Lucien. "I ain't a free man. I'm a trustee."

Lucien cocked an eye. "What the hell you say, Tom?"

"I'm doing time," Tom explained. "Got five years. The warden made me a trustee 'cause I can handle men and rigs. Life ain't so bad fer me. I don't sleep inside the wall. I got me a place a mile down the road. Built it myself. I take care of the warden's business, and the warden takes care of me."

"You're a damn convict?" Lucien asked bewildered.

"That's right, Mr. Lucien," Tom replied.

Lucien fumed and marched off. "I guess I'll kill the bastard myself!" he declared. "The first chance I get."

23.

Although it was mid-spring in Magnolia, it had not rained in weeks. Summer heat was coming on, and the sun blazed the land from dawn to dusk, leaving the ground dusty and dry. By afternoon, without benefit of a breeze, the hazy atmosphere often burned the eyes and made it difficult to see. Therefore, when Lucien Eliot drew up to Magnolia in his wagon, everyone squinted to watch him. He wore a hat pulled down over his forehead and a handkerchief tied across his face. Holding back on the reigns of his horses, he tried to keep down the dust. Going directly to the train depot, he found Silas unloading a wagon laden with eighty-pound bags of milled sugar. Lucien removed his hat and fanned his face. "Best do as I say," he said. "You know what I can do."

Silas wrung his hands. "Mr. Lucien," he began nervously. "You knows I works in the captain's house. He always been good to me. I got me a little house, and a title on it too. I can't do what you ask me. No, Mr. Lucien, I can't do that."

Lucien returned his hat to his head and tightened it down. "I understand, Silas," he said. "Some things a man's not prepared to do."

Silas quit wringing his hands, and grinned sheepishly. "I feel better now," he said. "Knowing you understand."

Lucien placed his hand in a brotherly fashion on the shoulder of Silas. "Bring that girl of yers by the house on Sunday. I'll put her to work in the kitchen. She can help some in my bedroom too. She'll look after me, and she'll give me some of the things a man needs."

"You talkin' 'bout Mable, my baby-girl?" asked Silas.

"Oh, she ain't a baby-girl," Lucien replied. "From what I can tell, she's all woman."

"Mr. Lucien, my—" Silas tried to speak, but Lucien cut him off by lifting his hand. "Just bring her by the house. If you don't, then I'll come get her."

Silas couldn't sleep that night, tossing and turning, agonizing over the thought of his baby-girl working in the house of Lucien. Although she was sixteen, Silas referred to her as his baby. Anyone, though, could see she was a woman, for she was pretty, and she had curves in the right places. Silas often worried about Mabel, for Magnolia was no place for a child. It had no school house, church or social organization. He had often considered asking McGeary to help Mabel go off to school somewhere, but he never got around to it. The truth was, he couldn't bear the thought of being without his daughter.

Silas stepped out of bed at first light, and he hiked two miles to McGeary's house. When he arrived, Cassandra was on the porch sweeping it clean with a straw broom.

"What's you doing here so early, Silas?" Cassandra asked. "Don't you know it's Sunday? Ain't nobody work on Sunday, except the women folk. Women folk work ain't never done."

"I come to see the captain."

"The captain sleep late on Sunday. But he be wakin' in a couple hours."

"I'll wait, Miz Cassandra."

"You wants something to eat while waitin'? How 'bout some fried eggs and a slab of bacon?"

"No, ma'am. I don't wants to be a bother."

"No bother. I got to go in the kitchen anyways. Me and the women folk gonna eat something. Then we gonna be fixin' a Sunday meal for the captain's family. You's invited, Silas. But eatin' won't be 'till afternoon. Best have something now."

"I just ain't hungry," said Silas.

Cassandra removed her apron and flapped it free of dust. "Suit yourself," she said.

Silas sat down on the steps of the porch and thought about his darling Mabel. She reminded him of her mother, a good woman who stayed with Silas through thick and thin. But then Silas got caught stealing bread from the local grocery, and the judge gave him a six-hundred-dollar fine or two years in prison if he couldn't pay it. His wife saw the situation as hopeless, and reaching her wit's end, she went up north alone, leaving Mabel with kin. A true sweetheart, Mabel scrawled letters to her father while he was a convict. As soon as Silas finished his prison sentence, he went to work for McGeary as a free man. He then sent for Mabel, and they became as close as ticks.

Shortly before noon, McGeary appeared in the archway to his house. Dressed in a silk robe, he seemed like a red-bearded sage. "What's so dang important, Silas, that you come here early on Sunday?"

Silas hung his head and rubbed his temples to loosen his distress. "It's my baby girl, Mabel."

"She sick?"

"No, she fine. But Mr. Lucien want to put her to work in his house."

"Why's he want Mabel to work at his place?"

"Ever'body know Lucien want to see you dead," Silas explained. "He figures I can help him. He says if I don't, he'll come take my baby-girl."

McGeary thoughtfully stroked his beard. "What exactly does Lucien want you to do?" he inquired.

"He wanna know the next time you go to the capital," replied Silas. "Ain't nobody know when you leaves out, except me, and your family too. I don't know what Lucien got in mind, but he he mad as hell, and no telling what he do."

"Let's have a morning meal," McGeary suggested. "It'll give me some time to figure this thing out. I don't think too good on an empty stomach."

Cassandra and Bessie prepared breakfast for the two men and served them in the kitchen. Silas merely dabbled with his food, but McGeary ate ravenously. Within fifteen minutes, he consumed six fried eggs, a bowl of grits, four biscuits and a pound of bacon. He concluded his meal with two cups of coffee and a chunk of chocolate.

McGeary cleaned his lips with a cloth napkin. "Silas," he began. "Listen to me carefully. Tell Lucien I'm going to the capital tomorrow. Tell him I'll board the train in Junction late afternoon."

"Why you gonna get the train in Junction?" Silas asked.

"Just do as I say," said McGeary.

Bessie delivered a pot of fresh coffee to the table, but the captain ignored it. He twisted his neck and peered about the kitchen, wondering if it were too early on a Sunday to have a shot of brandy.

24.

McGeary didn't board the train Junction as he told Silas he would, but he stayed at home most of the day. In the afternoon he went down to the depot, and he caught sight of Lucien waiting to board the train with Mack Davis, an ashen-faced hired gun from Kansas. McGeary watched Lucien as he paced the porch of the train office, puffing on a hand-rolled cigar while Davis picked his teeth with a splinter of wood. When the train arrived at three o'clock, McGeary kept out of sight and observed the pair from afar. He watched them step aboard the train. As it rolled out of the station, he chased it down and jumped aboard the last car. Peering cautiously inside, he didn't see Lucien or Davis, so he entered and took a seat.

Lucien was in a forward car, relaxing and seeming to be pleased with himself. "That damn McGeary thinks he's smart," Lucien told Davis. "But just wait till we get to Junction. He'll be dead before he steps aboard the train."

"Let me know when we get close to town," Davis said.

Lying his head back, he covered his eyes with his hat and slept.

In the rear car, McGeary remained vigilant, calmly waiting while the train wound the countryside for an hour. When the train was fifteen minutes outside of Junction, he stood up and strolled cavalierly down the aisle. Stepping into the forward car, he saw Lucien gazing out his window. McGeary reached into his holster, and lifting out his pistol, he kept it out of sight behind his back.

Lucien noticed McGeary coming down the aisle, and caught off guard he cried out, "It's god-damned McGeary!"

Davis abruptly awakened, and trying to direct his mind to control the situation, he saw McGeary aim his pistol. Lucien reached inside his coat and tried to remove his own weapon. However, in his haste, it got hung up with its holster, and though he desperately tried to wrench it free, he was unable to do so. McGeary, however, did not delay, and aiming with singular purpose, he shot Lucien in the chest. In an instant, McGeary let loose another shot, and it was a death blow, for it struck Lucien's forehead. Davis tried to push the corpse aside and free himself to draw his weapon.

"What are you gonna do?" asked McGeary, poking his pistol in Davis' face. "Wanna go for your gun?"

Davis was in a quandary to answer, and it took a moment for the fogginess in his head to clear. "You murdered Lucien Eliot!" he shouted. "You're a murderer, cold-blooded! I saw you shoot the man dead!"

"Yeah, the bastard's dead," said McGeary. "And you came close to being killed too."

"I'll see you hanged!" Davis declared.

McGeary glared at Davis. "Is that right?" he asked glibly. "You really think so?"

25.

The Sheriff of Junction was a young man named Barrister. In the heart of a woodsy county, not much happened here, and Sheriff Barrister had little to do, except on weekends when a logger occasionally got out of hand. He usually could be found weekdays in his office, the doors and windows wide open, his lawman's hat in hand, and his fingers shaping its oval brim. Thus he was surprised when a trio of citizen showed up at his office talking of a killing on the train. He hustled down to the station and began questioning witnesses. Not bothering to interrogate McGeary and Davis, he instead hauled them off to his office and placed them in separate cells.

"I saw everything, Sheriff," Davis spouted. "This man shot Mr. Eliot. He never gave the man a chance."

"What do you have to say for yourself?" the sheriff asked McGeary.

"Everybody knows Lucien wanted me dead," McGeary responded.

"That doesn't change anything," the sheriff snapped. "You shot a man who hadn't drawn his weapon. In the eyes of the law, that's manslaughter."

"Lucien saw me comin' down the aisle," McGeary calmly explained. "He shouted and awakened this fella here. I figure Lucien hired him. My bet is he's a hired gun."

The sheriff lifted a stubby pencil, and he set out a sheet of paper to write on. "What's your name, mister?" the sheriff asked.

"Addison McGeary."

"I know about you," the sheriff mused. "You're that fella from Magnolia."

"That's right."

The sheriff glanced over to the adjacent cell. "What's your name, mister?"

"Davis."

"Is that your Christian name?"

"No."

"Well, what *is* your Christian name?"

"Mack."

The sheriff scribbled the information on the sheet of paper. "Hummm, Mack Davis," Sheriff Bannister said, considering the name. "Sounds familiar."

"I guess I got a familiar-sounding name," said Davis. He sat on the cotton-stuffed mattress on his bunk and tested it for its hospitality.

The sheriff peered at Davis with a wary eye. "Is it true you were asleep when Mr. Eliot was shot?" he asked.

"I was awake and alert," Davis replied.

"Not according to witnesses," Sheriff Bannister said. "They say you were napping."

Davis tried to cover up his lie. "Well," he began. "Perhaps I dozed off for a moment or two. But the truth is, I saw McGeary murder Mr. Eliot."

McGeary spoke up in his own defense. "Lucien reached for his weapon," he said. "But it got hung up inside his coat."

"It's a lie!" cried Davis. "Mr. Eliot never saw him comin'. It was cold-blooded murder."

The sheriff turned to McGeary. "I guess it's your word against his," he explained.

"You gonna believe the word of a hired gun?" McGeary asked. "Or the word of a deputy sheriff?"

"Well, if I had my choice, I'd believe the deputy," the sheriff answered. "But I don't have a deputy as a witness."

McGeary reached into his shirt pocket. Lifting out his badge, he passed it through the bars to Sheriff Bannister. "Deputy Sheriff of Coastal City," said the sheriff, reading the face of the badge. "I'll have to check this out." He sighed and shook his head. "You fellas get comfortable," he added. "It might be awhile."

Left alone with McGeary, Davis began to banter. "Mr. Eliot told me about you. You was a coward during the war. You rode with the regulars out of Atlanta. I can't figure how you was a captain. You's a dirty, no-good coward."

"I imagine you were a bloody hero, right?"

"I killed my share of Yankees,"

McGeary remained composed, despite Davis tantalizing him. "I knows your kind," he began. "You likes ridin' into the killin' fields. You got a taste for blood. You like to do the burning of farms and homes. How 'bout the killin' of innocent folks, women and children?"

"I done what needed to be done. I wasn't no coward."

"I ain't one to judge a man. War can bring out evil in a fella. Like you say, some things had to be done. I did my share of killin' too. Before I rode with the regulars, I rode with Mobley's Raiders out of Missouri. I've no desire for blood now. But concernin' you, I'll make an exception. So make no mistake, if I see you within ten miles of Magnolia, I'll squash you like a roach."

"I don't think so," Davis said snidely. "You's a coward *and* a liar. You didn't ride with Mobley. His men was heroes. Blood-thirsty, but still they was heroes."

"On second thought," McGeary said. "I'll make you bleed real good, and then I'll tie you to a tree. Vultures will eat on your flesh. You can watch 'em pickin' your skin, and then they'll feast on your entrails."

Davis peered blankly into space, pretending not to take McGeary seriously. "Whatever you say," he said. "They's the words of a damn liar."

McGeary didn't speak any further. He simply sat on the edge of his bunk and patiently waited for the sheriff to return. Davis too, having purged himself of scorn, had nothing more to say. Silence swelled inside their cells, and coolly expanding, it filled the murky recesses of the sheriff's office.

26.

The door burst open an hour later, and Sheriff Bannister stepped through. "Well, I got the information I wanted," he said, his words directed toward Davis. "You'll be getting out of here soon. I just need to complete some paperwork."

"How long you think that'll be? Davis asked.

"Oh, sometime tomorrow, I suspect," the sheriff replied.

"Tomorrow?"

"Lot's of paperwork,"

Davis pointed at McGeary. "How about him?"

"He can leave now."

"What about me?"

"About you, well, I contacted authorities upstate. They tell me you're a hired gun. Folks in Junction don't much care for hired guns."

"Hell, lots of good men work as hired guns."

"A hired gun is one thing. A hired killer is another. You're an assassin, Mr. Davis. And I've got a notion to charge you with Intent to Commit Manslaughter. But I don't want you stinkin' up my office."

Sheriff Bannister unlocked McGeary's cell and set him free. "Let's have a drink, Deputy. Train doesn't leave for another two hours."

The saloon slept during the day, and the sheriff found it the perfect to escape for an afternoon smoke and a drink.

"What'll you have?" asked the sheriff, dragging a stool up to the bar for his guest. "How about a Scotch Whiskey?"

"Fine with me," replied McGeary.

The sheriff sauntered around the bar, and finding a silver-label bottle, he poured a pair of shots. Filling two tall glasses with beer from a keg beneath the bar, the men swallowed their Scotch in a single gulp, and then washed it down with a sudsy swig of beer.

The Scotch and the beer chaser promptly made Sheriff Bannister warm-headed. "You got quite a reputation," he said amicably to McGeary. "In Coastal City they say you're a bone-a-fide hero." McGeary leaned against the bar in silence, lingering like a stone statue. "You don't like talk much, do you?" the sheriff asked.

"Not as much as most," responded McGeary.

"Folks say I ask too many question," said the sheriff. "But a man in my position's always asking questions." McGeary nodded in agreement. "Maybe I shouldn't ask," the sheriff continued. "But I'd like to know about that storm in Coastal City. Folks say it was a nightmare."

"I don't recall much about it," McGeary replied. "I suspect it's best a man forgets some things." He took a long drink from his beer. Foam clung to his lips, and he wiped himself clean using a bar cloth. "I do remember one thing, though—the wind."

The sheriff inched over onto the edge of his barstool. "What about it?" he asked.

"It howled," said McGeary. "I thought it was the cries of the dyin'. But it wasn't. It was the waling of the storm. You see, Sheriff, the storm was alive, and I know it 'cause I could feel its breath. It was sometimes cool, and other times hot, like the devil hisself was breathing in and out."

"It must have been hell," commented the sheriff. "Pure hell."

"No, it wasn't hell," McGeary explained. "It was this world. It was our world."

27.

McGeary's dreams occurred more frequently. They began as they always did, with red rain flowing down like ribbons from heaven, but now there was more to the dreams. After the rain, the sun shone down and dried the land, leaving it crusty and littered with white stones. As McGeary looked over the landscape, he perceived that the stones were actually human skulls. Soldiers meandered among them, collecting the skulls and placing them in burlaps bags, which became hot and began to smolder. The scene suddenly changed, and McGeary saw smoke swirling. The atmosphere reeked with burning flesh, and the smell caused the soldiers to vomit and convulse.

McGeary abruptly awakened, sweat surging from his pores. Sitting up, he struck a match and lit a kerosene lamp beside the bed. Magdalena awakened to the lamp's light flickering on the walls of the room.

"The problem, what is?" she asked in her usual broken syntax.

McGeary rose from the bed, his head hung down and his shoulders slumped over. "I'll be fine," he mumbled.

Magdalena got up and crossed to her husband. She took his hand and held it. "You have bad dream," she said. "Tell me. Maybe I help you."

McGeary slipped his hand out of hers. "It ain't the kind of thing a man wants to share," he said. "Best to leave it alone." He then left the bedroom and unsteadily descended the stairway.

Magdalena called out from the top of the stairs. "You not can run from bad dreams!" she cried, holding her robe closely to her body with her fist. "You not can run!"

Cassandra was awakened by the commotion, and she hurriedly got out of bed to find out what happened.

"He have bad dreams," Magdalena explained. "He no will talk to me." She implored Cassandra to help her. "What I can do? Tell me, please, what I can do?"

"Ain't nothin' nobody can do," Cassandra replied. "The captain know too much sin."

"Sin?" asked Magdalena mystified. "What sin my husband do?"

"Ain't nobody know," Cassandra replied. "The captain's sin belong to him, and ain't nobody's business." She wrapped her arm about Magdalena's waist, and she led her away. "Best you leave him be. The captain want to be alone."

Magdalena grudgingly returned to her room. Getting into her bed, she slipped in between the satin sheets, and curling up into herself, she sobbed.

28.

A stroke of cool wind came in from the northwest, and the women in McGeary's household, soapy fresh from their morning baths, shuttled about the house humming and singing. McGeary and Magdalena were in the sitting room, relaxing and sipping black coffee. They spoke of nothing important, merely of domestic things; that is until Magdalena brought up the subject of her brother, whom McGeary called "Little Tim" because he couldn't pronounce his indigenous name.

"He is seven years now," Magdalena said. "He need school. All childs need school."

"We don't have a schoolhouse," said McGeary. "And even if we did, we don't have a school teacher." McGeary stood, and he adjusted his belt to conform to his stomach. "I best be gettin' along. There's work to be done."

McGeary walked outdoors to a horse-drawn wagon, but before he hopped aboard, he noticed someone walking over the far ridge. He couldn't discern who it was, but he was certain it a free man. McGeary stood beside his wagon and hung around waiting. When the man got close enough to be recognized, McGeary sounded off.

"That you, Henry?" he asked. "Henry Fields?"

Henry got closer. "Yes, sir," he replied. "It's me, Captain."

The two men shook hands firmly. "What you doin' back here?" asked McGeary. "I figured you to have more sense than to come back to this hell hole."

"Magnolia is no hell hole," Henry replied. "It's sheer Paradise!"

McGeary bellowed with laughter, and once his jollity subsided, he took Magdalena by the hand. "This is my wife, Magdalena," he said, proudly introducing the young beauty.

"Nice to meet you," said Henry.

"Nice to meet you," Magdalena echoed.

"She's a great cook," McGeary said, draping his arm over Henry's shoulders. "Let's make you something to eat. You look like you can use a good meal. A man's never had eggs and beefsteak until he's had 'em smothered in chili peppers."

In the kitchen, Magdalena took control of the cooking while Bessie squeezed fruit to prepare cool refreshments.

"What brings you back to Magnolia, Henry?" asked McGeary.

The spicy peppers simmered in a pan, and the pungent scent filled the air. The aroma appeared to make Henry woozy. "Well, since you killed Mr.—" Henry began. "I mean since Mr. Eliot passed on, I thought I'd come back to Magnolia."

McGeary thoughtfully massaged the back of his neck with his hand. "What you gonna do?" he asked in a puzzled tone. "You gonna work the cane fields for seven dollars a month? An educated man like you might earn fifty in Atlanta."

"I'm a preacher now," Henry replied. "A preacher goes where he's needed, and folks in Magnolia need a preacher."

"I won't argue with that," said McGeary. "But Magnolia ain't no place to live. Someday it'll grow into a town. For now, though, it's just a village." McGeary believed he had gotten his idea through to Henry, and he figured to put a nail in it. "A preacher can't hold church services in a cane field."

"That's why I came here this morning, Captain. I thought I'd ask your help."

"How's that?"

"I need some board timber to build a church. The congregation will do the building, and we'll all pay you for the board-timber from the offering plate."

McGeary considered Henry's proposition like any other business matter. "How many folks you have now in your congregation?"

"Oh, perhaps twenty men—some with families. But the congregation will grow." Magdalena set a plate of fried eggs and peppered beefsteak in front of Henry. He admired the meal as if it were a work of art. "The congregation will pay you back, Captain. I promise."

"Enjoy your meal, Henry. We'll talk business later."

The preacher cut into the peppered beefsteak and sliced off a piece. Inserting the spicy meat into his mouth, he chewed for a moment and then swallowed. "That's not bad," he mused. "In fact, it's quite good."

The compliment caused Magdalena to smile.

Once Henry had finished eating, McGeary picked up the conversation where the two men left off. "I imagine every congregation needs a roof and four walls," he said. "Perhaps I can help out."

"You're a generous man," said Henry.

"Maybe, maybe not," responded McGeary. "I got an offer for you." Henry inclined forward and listened. "If you help me out with a small problem I got, I'll not only provide board-timber for a church, but also for a schoolhouse."

"A schoolhouse?" Henry asked, thrilled with the idea. "What exactly do I need to do?"

"Well, you see, I've got this....." McGeary began, but he soon paused. Little Tim was on his mind. The odd thing was, he didn't know how to reference the boy, for in fact, Little Tim was his brother-in-law. "I have this *boy*," McGeary opted to say. "He needs educatin'. He don't speak much English—only a few words here and there. I don't understand him none, and he don't understand me."

"What language does the boy speak?" Henry asked.

"That's hard to figure," replied McGeary. "His mama's a half-breed, and his pa's a full-blood Yaqui Indian."

"Then her parents need to learn English too," Henry presumed.

McGeary took pause, and lifting a sugar bowl, he studied it as if searching for a defect in its workmanship. "I got nothin' against Indians," he finally said. "Her parents don't care none for learnin' English. They ain't the smartest folks in the world. But her pa sure knows about growin' a garden. We got bushels of tomatoes, peppers, sweet onions, grapes, strawberries....."

"Strawberries?" asked Henry.

"Sweet, fat, and juicy," replied McGeary. "Her pa works magic in a garden."

"Are you trying to bribe me? asked Henry.

"Of course, I am," McGeary replied.

Henry considered the proposition. "A schoolhouse for one small boy doesn't make sense," he stated.

"What are you tryin' to say?" asked McGeary. "That you don't want a schoolhouse?"

"No, a schoolhouse is fine," Henry replied. "I'm just thinking about all the children of convicts that need an education."

"Well, teach them too," McGeary suggested. "They need educatin' like everybody else."

"So, if I teach this young boy," Henry said, intending to clarify McGeary's proposal. "You'll buy the board-timber needed to build both a church and a schoolhouse?"

"That's correct," McGeary affirmed.

"Well, perhaps we can agree on that," Henry said. "But being both a schoolmaster and a church pastor can make for a lot of work. I'll have expenses, buying books and such."

"Are you negotiating with me?" asked McGeary.

"Yes, sir, I am," Henry confessed.

"Then I'll pay you a salary," said McGeary with an air of finality. "Somethin' to help you pay expenses."

"How much salary?" asked Henry.

"Oh, say, thirty-five dollars per month," McGeary replied.

"Make it fifty dollars," said Henry.

"Hummm," McGeary muttered. "For fifty dollars you got to give my wife private lessons. She knows to speak English some, but she can use your help, especially with readin' and writin'."

Henry agreed to the terms, and the two men shook hands.

29.

Nobody but Bessie James knew why Wilkie split his shackles with a stone wedge and ran off toward freedom. For the time present, McGeary didn't much care, for he angrily dashed off in his wagon, a pair of shotguns at his feet, and Silas sitting beside him.

"Wilkie sure be crazy," Silas said. "He was down-low too long. I ain't never been down-low. And now that I's a free man, I won't never be. Down-low don't mean nothin' to Wilkie. I imagine it done made him crazy."

A horseman came out of the cane fields and galloped toward the wagon. It was Ole Tom. He carried two pistols inside his belt, and on his saddle hung a tightly braided leather whip. "We got Wilkie James," Ole Tom announced. "Heading for the river." He held his head up, proud as a peacock. "What ya want we do?"

"Take me to him," ordered McGeary. "I wanna talk with this crazy convict."

Wilkie was held two miles down river, watched over by a quintet of prison guards and convict trustees. His arms and legs were securely bound, and he sat on the ground with his knees supporting his head. He looked nothing like a belligerent convict, for his soul was utterly exhausted, and his body begged to rest.

Once McGeary arrived, he stepped down from his wagon, and he stood over Wilkie like a colossus. "Take his shackles off," McGeary ordered the guards.

"Captain, he's loco," Ole Tom said. "No tellin' what he'll do."

"You got shotguns," commented McGeary. "Even a crazy Negro knows what a shotgun can do to a man."

Once his shackles were removed, Wilkie lifted his head and surveyed his captives, staring up at them with gritty eyes.

"Stand up, boy," McGeary demanded. Wilkie ignored the command and folded his arms across his chest in an act of defiance. "Don't you know who I am?" asked McGeary. "I'm the man who says if you die or live. You ain't so crazy as to wanna die, are you?" Wilkie lifted himself up from the ground, and he stood face to face with McGeary. He was not as tall as the captain, but the muscles in his arms and neck were as big as any McGeary had seen. "What's the matter with you?" McGeary asked him. "Why don't you do what's right?" Wilkie wrinkled his forehead. "Don't get crazy with me," McGeary advised. "I'm the man can give you a two-room shanty, and maybe a few acres. Every man wants his own land. You do what's right. I give you what you want." Wilkie nixed the captain. "You know what I gots to do now," McGeary added. "I gotta give you the lash. 'Cause if I don't, the other convicts gonna say I'm weak."

Ole Tom tossed McGeary his whip. A pair of guards grasped Wilkie by his wrists, and they bound them by a length of rope. The guards then pushed Wilkie's face against a tree, and they tightened his hands around its trunk. McGeary ripped Wilkie's shirt from his shoulders and exposed his back, which was disfigured by the whips of other men. He then took a position ten feet away from Wilkie, and he snapped his whip at the base of Wilkie's neck. The convict did not react, but he simply stood strong to receive his flogging. McGeary cracked the lash once more, but still, Wilkie did not react. He accepted the pain, storing it away somewhere deep in the core of his soul.

McGeary never knew a man not to flinch at the stroke of a whip, and the fact that Wilkie was able to do it angered him. He thrashed once more, and blood dripped from Wilkie's shoulders. McGeary continued lashing, Ole tom counting out five, ten, and then twenty. McGeary experienced a nauseating feeling in the pit of his stomach, and he became dizzy. His world began to spin, and soon he fell away. As he lay on the ground, memories of the war returned to him, like seasons in their time, opening the doors of his mind to a world he had tried to forget. He lay on the ground semi-conscious, hearing muttering voices above him. Silas rushed to McGeary with a gourd of water, and poured out a soothing stream onto McGeary's forehead and face. The captain, however, did not awaken, for his vital energies had fled from his spirit. Ole Tom and a prison guard lifted McGeary onto the bed of his wagon, and Silas took the horse's reigns. With a single snap of a carriage whip, the wagon hurried away.

Once Silas arrived at McGeary's place, the entire household rushed out of the house, astonished to see the man they perceived as invincible lying lifelessly in the wagon. Magdalena let out a maddening scream, and it became necessary for the household women to take hold of her. "He's dying!" Magdalena cried out. "Somebody help. Please, help him!"

Cassandra took hold of Magdalena, and stared into her face with black, scintillating eyes. "I takes care of things," she said, trying to reassure the young woman. "You don't worry none. I do what needs be done."

Helped by two of the women, Silas carried McGeary upstairs to his bedroom and placed him in his bed. He lay listlessly, heavily breathing and murmuring unintelligible things.

Cassandra went to the kitchen and broke seven eggs open on the rim of a bowl. Returning to McGeary's bedroom, she chased everyone out, except for Magdalena, who refused to leave her husband.

"I'll stay until he wakes," she said adamantly.

Cassandra acquiesced, and she commanded Magdalena to sit back and not to speak. She then dipped her hands into the eggs and slowly withdrew them, her fingers dripping with sticky, organic matter. She rubbed the substance onto McGeary's scalp and flesh, covering all parts of his neck and face. Magdalena became drowsy from watching, and she fell into deep sleep. Cassandra proceeded with her ritual, but now she applied the runny eggs to McGeary's chest and legs, continuing until the bowl was empty, and McGeary's spirit quieted.

30.

A full day passed before McGeary awakened. It was an hour before dawn, and a silvery moon hung in the sky. He sat up in bed, his thoughts drifting without purpose. He didn't know how long he slept, nor did he know how he arrived to his room. However, such mundane details seemed unimportant now, and he didn't bother with finding answers.

Descending the stairs, he arrived to the kitchen, and peeking inside the adjoining room where Bessie kept her bed, he saw her slumbering. "I'm sorry," he whispered to her from afar. "I'm truly sorry."

The captain then walked out of the kitchen and found the sitting room, which was moonlit and shadowed. In the solace of early morn, he relaxed in a cushioned chair and nodded off. Minutes later he awakened to Bessie's lips kissing his hand.

"Forgive me what I done, Captain," Bessie begged, her knees down on the floor. "I should a said somethin'. Wilkie's mama been sick. I knowed what he was gonna do. But I was prayin' the lord to help. It be too late now. Wilkie's mama dead. I made a mess of ever'thing. Best you send me away. I got too much shame on me. I can't rightly face nobody. Send me away, Captain. You gots to send me away."

McGeary ached at the sight of Bessie on her knees. "I won't be sending you off," he said, lifting her hand and motioning for her to stand. "You're a part of my family." His words had an effect of healing on Bessie, and she suddenly felt free from her anguish. "Go on into the kitchen," McGeary told her. "Cook me up a beefsteak. I'm mighty hungry."

Bessie dried her eyes. "Yes, Captain. I cook you the best beefsteak you ever ate."

31.

After his early morning meal, Captain McGeary sat by a window and looked out passed the laced curtains that were slightly parted, allowing him to see the windowpane that dripped with morning dew. He sat trance-like, waiting for the sun to rise above the trees, to warm the window and dry the beads of condensation. After the sun rose up, he remained alone in the room, mostly all day, isolated from his family and detached from all things worldly. When evening drew nigh, he boarded his wagon and headed for the schoolhouse where he hoped to find Henry.

Unknown to McGeary, Henry was a mile away, sitting with Silas on the front steps of Silas' two-room shanty. The two men were at ease together, talking about the church and how it was growing. They also spoke about Mabel and her receiving letters from a boy back home. It seemed to Silas that one day they'd get married, and the fact appeared to make him happy. Silas excused himself, and going inside the house, he promptly returned with a bottle of brandy.

"How bout a drink, Henry?" asked Silas.

"I'm a preacher," Henry replied. "Preachers try to stay away from liquor."

"Suit yourself," said Silas. He took a swallow and set the brandy down. Henry lifted the bottle and read its label. "Imported from France. "This is fine brandy."

"I imagine so. It be from the captain's cabinet."

Henry frowned and sounded a lament. "I'm disappointed, Silas. You shouldn't thieve the captain's best liquor."

"I didn't thieve nothin', The captain give it to me."

Henry lifted the bottle by the neck, and he peered through the glass to examine the clear amber liquid inside it. Dipping his pinky finger inside the rim of the bottle, he withdrew it and dabbed it on his lip. He realized immediately that the brandy was of superior vintage. Henry decided to surrender himself to temptation. "Maybe I'll have just one drink. Lord knows even a preacher gets thirsty."

Silas smiled expansively, happy that Henry decided to join him in a drink. A few gulps later, when the brandy had sufficiently relaxed him, Silas reached inside his shirt and withdrew a fat cigar. Snapping it in half with his hands, he passed a section to Henry, and he kept the other part for himself. "I don't knows much 'bout tobacco," Silas confessed. "But the captain's cigars smoke real good. He call 'em something. I can't remembers the word, but its sounds like 'bananas'."

Henry was amused and laughed blithely. "Havanas," corrected Henry. "From Cuba—best tobacco in the world."

Silas struck a match on a stone, and he got his half of the cigar started. "Yeah, best in the world," Silas said, endorsing Henry's opinion. "The captain be good to me."

Henry was suspicious by nature, and once again he questioned Silas' ethics. "I can't believe the captain would give away such a fine cigar."

"He give me a fist full of 'em," Silas declared. "I still gots one inside the house. I keeps it in a little wood box. Captain says that's how they's kept fresh."

Hearing this, Henry plummeted into deep thought. "Hummmm" he moaned.

Silas interpreted his friend's conduct as a cause for concern. "What's on your mind, Henry?" Silas asked.

Henry responded straightforwardly. "I'm thinking I'll rest from being a preacher this evening," he replied, tossing aside all his worries. "Best I relax and have a good smoke as well as a fine brandy."

It was Silas' turn to laugh. "You always say The Good Lord provides," Silas declared. "He just sometime provide by the captain's hand."

The two friends chatted mirthfully, and after awhile they noticed a wagon roll up the dirt road that led to Silas' shanty. In the twilight the image was merely an outline, and it wasn't until the image drew closer did they see that it was Captain McGeary. His wagon rattled up to the house, and the three men bid each other good evening. McGeary got out the wagon and lingered leisurely, eyeing a cluster of stars above. Breathing in the night air, he seemed reinvigorated.

"It's a magnificent evening," McGeary announced.

"What brings you out this way, Captain?" asked Silas. "I don't get many visitors out here, except for Preacher Henry."

"I figured to go for a ride," McGeary answered. "And I found myself comin' out to your place."

"Well, we're glad you came," Henry enthused.

McGeary continued standing, listening to the crackling of crickets and the caw of crows in the fields. "How's that church of yours doin'?" he asked Henry.

"Just fine. The congregation's got nearly twenty-five dollars saved up, and we're about to make our first payment on that board-timber."

"Don't worry none 'bout paying me for the board-timber. You just keep on preachin' to folks."

Silas and Henry exchanged furtive glances, for they knew McGeary rarely capitulated in matters of business.

"How 'bouts a drink?" Silas offered. "I gots a clean glass inside the house."

Silas moved to stand, but McGeary gestured for him to sit. "Just pass the brandy." Receiving the bottle, McGeary took a hearty drink. Returning the bottle to Silas' hands and noticed the cigar Silas puffed on. "That one of my Havanas?"

Preacher Henry shrank from the question, but his conscience compelled him to speak. "Silas says you gave it to him."

McGeary was in a temperate mood, and therefore he maintained civility. "I must have been drunk."

"Oh, you was, Captain. You hardly could get up the stairs. You say to me, 'Silas, gets me up to my room.' So I helps you, and when we gets there, you opens a box of cigars and gives me a fist full of 'em."

McGeary was unable to recall the event. However, he gave Silas the benefit of the doubt. "It's good that I gives you some Havanas. You got any more of 'em? I'm in the mood for a smoke myself."

Silas' eyes brightened gregariously. "In the house, Captain." He stood up and charged through the doorway, quickly returning with a cigar. "It be whole and not been broke. You smoke all you wants, Captain."

McGeary lit the Havana and smoked it. Puckering his lips, he blew out a perfectly formed smoke ring. "Henry, I been meanin' to ask you somethin'. How many convicts you figure I got on lease?"

Henry scratched his chin with his fingers. "Three-hundred souls, I imagine," he replied.

"And how many of them are murders," McGeary asked. "Or evil men who done violent things?"

"Convicts like that the warden puts down-low," replied Henry. "The men that go on lease are mostly good men."

"What are you saying?" asked McGeary.

Henry nudged Silas with his elbow. It was an inquiring nudge that asked for his help in explaining things.

Silas got the message. "Ever'body know," he began. "Most colored convicts did little nothin'. Sheriff picks 'em up and the judge gives 'em a fine. If they can't pay, they goes to prison. Mostly that means goin' out on lease." Silas realized that he had unwillingly disparaged McGeary. "It ain't you," he assured the captain. "But the judge is doin' the wrong. The sheriff too. Convicts don't mind workin' the cane fields. It be better than working the mines."

McGeary was unsure about Silas' use of the word *mines.* "Mines?" he asked.

"Coal mines," Henry explained. "Rumor is there's a dozen coal mines. All of them worked by Negro convicts."

The captain tried to set the record straight. "Leasing of convicts is a good thing," he said. "No reason why the government should pay for a man's transgressions. If a convict wants a good meal, then he should work for it—same as a free man."

"Yes, sir, Captain," Henry agreed. "There's one problem, though. Many Negroes are sent to prison for vagrancy and other small crimes. Those working the mines eat and sleep in the bowels of the earth. They rarely come up, not for sunshine or fresh air. After a year or two, they die there. They're buried in unmarked graves somewhere above ground where nobody can find them. No telling how many Negroes die in the mines."

The idea was incredulous to McGeary. "Lots of folk talk, Henry," he said. "It's mostly rumors started by old women and folks that got no sense."

"Don't take my word for it," said Henry. "Ask Wilkie James. He's one of the few men who worked the mines and lived to tell about it."

"That's right, Captain," Silas said, ringing in with support for Henry. "Wilkie know all 'bout the mines. He got sent to for picking up peaches on the road."

McGeary propped himself against the rail of the shanty's porch and resumed smoking. "Henry, tomorrow you and Silas come with me," he said. "We'll go talk to Wilkie James."

Silas bowed up, and his eyes got big. "Wilkie be inside the wall," he said. "I don't wants to go back there. I best forget that place."

McGeary looked to Henry. "What about you?" the captain asked. "The prison got you scared?"

Henry thought about it. "I'm not afraid of the prison," he replied. "But frankly, I don't want to step inside the place."

32.

She prayed for him, Bessie for Crazy Wilkie, and he became uncrazy, his anger falling away, leaving him content and resolved to his fate. It was not a gradual change that came over the man, but an instantaneous one. He didn't even realize it happened, because outwardly his days continued the same. He trudged along with other convicts, going in and out of the cane fields, laboring until late afternoon and returning to prison before nightfall. Yet it was obvious to everyone who knew Wilkie that he had made a change; he had shed his old self and become visibly different, like a serpent sheds its skin, revealing a fresh outfit for a new season.

When Bessie learned of her husband's transformation, she pranced light-footed about McGeary's house, joyfully praising The Lord. "There's power in the blood," she cried out. "Power in the blood." Her bliss was contagious among the other women of the household, and they shared Bessie's happiness by singing spirit-filled songs.

"I don't believe it," the captain said to Silas. "No man changes like folks say Wilkie did." The two men sat inside McGeary's home office, a small area sandwiched between the kitchen and the living room. "How do you account for it, Silas?"

"It was Bessie's doin'," Silas replied. "She be sayin' there's power in the blood. The Lord is mighty, that's fer sure."

McGeary shuffled through a stack of papers on his desk. "I seen men find The Lord one day, and the next day find the bottle. We gonna have to wait to and see 'bout Wilkie."

Cassandra entered the room with a pitcher of iced tea. "Something cool to drink, Captain? How about you, Silas?" She emptied the picture into a pair of tall drinking glasses. "It not be too sweet. I hopes you like it."

"What do ya think about Wilkie James?" McGeary asked her. "The change come over him is hard to believe, ain't it?"

Cassandra became solemn. "Some things be hard to believe," she responded. "I seen lots of strange things. I even seen folks waken from the dead."

McGeary remained suspect. "Did you give Wilkie James a potion?" he asked.

"No, Captain," Cassandra replied. "Bessie would hear nothing of it. She told me The Lord gonna take care of things. And I imagine he did. If we believe, Bessie say, we can move a mountain. That was some mountain got moved. Sure was."

33.

At the end of each month, as was McGeary's obligation, he visited the prison to give his lease payment to the warden. He climbed the tightly-wound circular stairs leading to the room outside the warden's office, being careful not to bump his forehead against the steps above. When he surfaced, he noticed a gentleman in a Panama hat sitting outside the warder's office. His name was Stanton, and he was a big name in behind-the-scene state politics. He was the man who dangled carrots and pulled strings. He got candidates re-elected to office, and he got friendly new-comers financed. When a vote came up on the floor of the legislature, he made sure it went his way. He passed money around generously, perpetually increasing his interests in hotels, minerals, land, and cattle.

"Warden's out and about," said Stanton, smoothing out the wrinkled lapels of his white linen suit. "Taking care of prison business, I guess. I heard him say something about a dead colored boy, and some place called down-low. No telling what the hell that is." McGeary sat on a stool at the opposite side of the room. Folding his hands atop his belly, he began to tap his thumbs together. It was not a nervous gesture, but rather a sign of detachment. "Is it true that you're one hell of a poker player," asked Stanton. "What's your secret?"

McGeary quit tapping his thumbs. "Ain't no secret," he said. "Poker's like anything else. You got to be lucky."

Stanton didn't altogether agree, for he knew gambling was more than mere luck. But before he could proffer a comment, he heard the warden thumping up the stairs.

The instant the warden stepped onto the second floor, he saw the two men seated in the room outside his office. "This is a coincidence," the warden commented. "The two men I wanted to get together with." The warden swept his hand chivalrously in the direction of his office. "Step inside, gentleman. Let's have a talk."

The group had hardly gotten through the door when the warden began to discourse. "Mr. Stanton has purchased Lucien Eliot's tract," he began. "He plans to grow cane. Naturally, he's come to me about leasing convicts. Mr. Stanton also needs a good man to manage his interests. I recommended you, Captain McGeary. You're the best in the cane business, and besides, you two men are going to be neighbors."

Stanton puffed himself up. "I plan on cultivating 30,000 acres of sugarcane," he explained. "And someday soon I'll build a refinery. Folks back East prefer white, granulated sugar, and they'll pay a good price for it. With the Snake River and the Mid-West Southern running through the region, we'll make millions." McGeary raised his eye brows, a gesture that seemed to suggest his interest. "So, what do you think?" Stanton asked.

"It's something to consider," McGeary replied. "I always said that big money's to be made in cane."

Stanton quickly cut through the chaff. "Then it's simply a matter of coming to terms," he said. "I figure to be generous. With both Eliot's tract and yours, I calculate we'll turn an annual profit of more than three-hundred-thousand dollars. We'll divide the profits equally."

The warden was impressed. "That's a pretty penny," he said, encouraging McGeary to agree. "On a monthly basis, your part might be as much as fifteen-thousand dollars."

McGeary contemplated Stanton's proposal, but he wanted more details. "I wonder," he said. "What'd you pay for the Eliot tract?"

"Eliot's estate went into the hands of a probate judge," Stanton replied. "He ordered the tract sold at auction. I was high bidder at forty-thousand dollars. However, I've had additional expenses of thirty thousand. Things don't get done in the capital without passing around some cash."

Leaning back on the edge of his desk, the warden spoke emphatically. "Yeah, I know that better than anybody."

McGeary nodded his head business-like, but he wasn't agreeable to Stanton's proposal. "Magnolia already turns an annual profit of more than one-hundred thousand," he explained. "I got a clear title on the land, mills, stock and warehouses. Magnolia is enough for any one man. I see no need for workin' 30,000 acres more."

Stanton was disappointed. He removed a handkerchief from his pocket, and he mopped his neck clean of sweat. "I won't try to change your mind, McGeary," he said. "You know what's best for you and yours. All the same, I need a good man, and a good man is hard to find."

"The best field manager I know is Ole Tom," said McGeary. "He knows how to run men and rigs, and he also knows cane."

The warden pushed back a few strands of his oily hair and tucked them behind his ears. "Ole Tom is a convict," he informed Stanton. "He's trusted, though, and like the captain says, he knows men and rigs. But he's doing time."

"If this convict is as competent as you say he is," said Stanton. "Then I've no problem with him managing the fields. Sales and distribution is another thing, though."

McGeary had a suggestion. "There's plenty smart fellas in the capital who can handle that part of the business," he hinted. "But if I was you, I'd sell the Eliot tract and turn a nice profit. You brought it for seventy-thousand dollars, and now you might could sell the place for four-hundred-thousand."

"Are you a buyer, Mr. McGeary?"

"Not at all," the captain replied. "Like I say, Magnolia is enough for any man."

"I wish you'd reconsider."

"I won't do that. But I'll give you rights of free access to the Snake River and the Mid-West Southern freight depot in Magnolia."

"That's a kind offer. And I'll also take your suggestion under advisement. Perhaps it's best to sell the Eliot tract and turn a quick profit."

Stanton departed, and the warden was left alone with McGeary. "I never met a man quite like you, Captain. You're hard to figure, but you talk straight, and I respect that. I was hoping that you and Stanton would come to an agreement. It'd be nice to have more convicts out on lease."

"You'll soon have 'em, soon enough. Stanton's probably on his way to the telegraph office, contacting potential buyers. For the time being, you're gonna find something extra in my lease payment."

The warden expressed his thanks, and he expected McGeary to exit, but the captain sat down on a chair. The warden did the same, slipping into his swivel chair behind his desk. "So, what's on your mind, Captain?"

"I was just thinking. You seem to be a decent fella."

"As decent as a prison warden can be."

"Yeah, well, that's somethin' troublin' me. Convicts ain't treated so decently at the prison. But I don't treat 'em so decent in the fields either. I guess being tough is the best way to handle dangerous men." McGeary paused and stroked his beard. "They are dangerous, aren't they?"

The warden defended himself. "Convicts here are treated better than in other places. They could be on lease in the mines, working in the bowels of earth. In the mines, convicts are treated worse than animals."

"So, it's true. There's mines up north."

"Yeah," the warden acknowledged. Leaning back in his chair, he appeared unwilling to further talk about the mines.

McGeary stood up, and he placed his hands on the warden's desk like a veteran statesman. "I done things I'm shamed of.

Horrible things I won't never speak. I wish I could change what I done, but I can't. I won't never forget neither. I won't never get free from the past. The future is another thing, though. A man can change the future."

"Where's this conversation leading?" asked the warden.

"Wilkie James," McGeary replied. "I'm thinkin' to make him a free man."

The warden huffed. "Don't believe that crap about him becoming a changed man," the warden advised. Peering at McGeary, he saw determination, and therefore he decided to plainly explain the reality of the situation. "Wilkie has fines to be paid, like most other convicts. The judge wasn't easy on him. He was in trouble before. First time was for larceny. He served his time in a coal mine up north. He was one of the few who ever got set free. He was a tough, hard-working young man, and the warden had pity on him. But when he went home, he soon got picked up for vagrancy. Wilkie didn't take it lightly, and he broke the jaw of a deputy. The judge figured to send him away for awhile. He gave Wilkie three years, and a three-thousand-dollar fine. He's served most of his time, but he still owes on his fine."

"How much exactly?" McGeary asked.

"You're serious about this, aren't you?"

"How much?"

"Wilkie's been so much trouble I've a mind to let you have him for nothing."

"That's generous of you."

McGeary marched toward the door and promptly exited. The warden realized what he'd done, for his intention wasn't to free Wilkie without his fine getting paid, but he merely wanted to extend the captain a discount. It was impossible now to take back his words, and all he could do was relax and to mumble. "Good luck with Wilkie James, Captain. He's one crazy Negro."

34.

The captain received word by telegraph that the new buyers of Eliot's land were coming in, and they wanted to meet their neighbor. He was hospitable to them, sending a carriage to the train station and inviting them out to the house for drinks and dinner. The new buyers accepted, and when they arrived, Cassandra ushered them into the sitting room where McGeary waited.

"I'm Clint Madison and this is my partner Sol Fleshman."

McGeary firmly shook their hands, and he motioned for them to sit down. "Brandy or whiskey?"

"Brandy's fine."

"We feel like we know you," said Clint, reaching across a polished tea table for a brandy glass. "Awhile back, Lucien Eliot came to us looking for investors to purchase your place. You had a change of mind about selling, and I can't say I blame you. Stanton says Magnolia turns a nice profit."

"I've been lucky," said McGeary. "But it's hard work that makes the luck."

"You're the kind of man we'd like to do business with," said Sol Fleshman. "How would you like to be our partner?" he asked.

"It's something to consider," replied McGeary.

Clint Madison pursued the issue, trying to sell McGeary on the idea. "We've got clear title on Eliot's tract, and an option to purchase forty-thousand acres more northwest of here. We're going to tear down that old wood-frame ramshackle of a courthouse and build one of brick and stone. The state's agreed to pick up most of the cost. South Fort County won't be a frontier much longer."

"It's on its way into the twentieth century," Sol Fleshman boasted. "It'll be an important center for big business."

"That's all well and good," said McGeary. "But I'm just a country boy. I don't know much about politics or big business. I only know about two things—poker and cane."

Clint Madison upped the ante. "We're willing to give you a sweetener of fifty-thousand dollars in cash," he said. "We'll form an equal partnership, and we'll join the Eliot and Magnolia Tracts into one operation."

"You'll find that we deal fairly," added Sol Fleshman. "We ask that you manage all the important affairs, and to take of the *necessary* things that need to be done."

McGeary was curious. "What are the *necessary* things?" he asked.

"Everybody knows how tough it is dealing with Negro convicts," Clint explained. "If something needs to be done, do it quietly. Bury the bodies somewhere in the sugar fields. The last thing we want is the Federals snooping around."

The comment sifted in McGeary's his mind. "Have another drink, gentlemen," McGeary said. "Then we'll eat a few beefsteaks."

During the meal, Sol Fleshman returned to the subject of business. "We're looking forward to having you for a partner."

McGeary didn't bother to look up from his plate. "I don't think so, gentlemen. I don't much care for partners. Like I told Stanton, Magnolia already turns a nice profit."

Bessie entered the room wearing a frilled apron. "I mades pecan pie. And we still gots some black-bean coffee. I grinds it fresh when you folks be ready."

"I'll be neighborly, gentlemen," McGeary said, chomping down on a portion of meat. "You'll find me a generous man. But as far as my havin' partners, I'm not interested."

35.

Madison and Fleshman were right about the future. The state built a new courthouse in South Fort County. Constructed of brick and sandstone, it was equal in statue to most any courthouse in the state. Sugarcane business in the county was becoming increasingly profitable, and many new opportunities presented themselves. Madison and Fleshman took advantage of them wherever possible. McGeary, though, stayed away from the county seat, and he tended to his business in Magnolia.

McGeary appointed Silas and Wilkie as his personal emissaries to his convict field-hands. Each new arrival to the cane fields got a stern talk on how to conduct themselves, and in this manner they were oriented into McGeary's program.

"You work hard," Silas told all the newcomers. "Someday Captain brings you outside the wall—gives you a shanty to live in. Your kin come be with you. But you gots to work dawn to dusk, so Captain knows you be a convict he can trust."

Most convicts listened and worked diligently, while others, unwilling to believe in the promise of a white man, ignored Silas' advice. They instead indulged themselves in an opposing dream, like escape from prison life. To those rebellious souls, Silas had a distinct message.

"The warden send you down-low. No telling how long you stays. Best you be dead, though, 'cause down-low be for slow dyin'. No man wanna be that way. You ask Wilkie James."

Sometimes a convict needed Wilkie's personal testimony. Wilkie would cleverly take his time, chatting with the man about small things and gaining his confidence. Then, when time came to rest awhile, Wilkie would sit with the convict in the shade of a tree, and he would reveal the stark reality of things.

"Down-low be a hole in the ground, 'cept there be ten, twenty men inside. They all be chained. They sleeps and eats in that hole. Never sees the sunshine. When they got bowels that need release, they squats down. Makes an awful stink. But that stink ain't so bad as the stink of dead men. Dead-man stink make you ache, make you vomit, and sick, 'til you too be dyin', and when you be dead they don't come for you 'til Sunday, drags you out and buries you outside the wall someplace nobody know. If Ole Tom ask you if you wants the lash or go down-low, you say you wants the lash. I be knowin' the lash, and I be knowing down-low. Ain't no place like down-low 'cept maybe hell. I be here now 'cause my Bessie pray for me. The Captain bring me out. Now I be free."

Henry's schoolhouse grew by leaps and bounds, and his church congregation got bigger as well. Henry was fond of saying that every child needs a grammar-school education, and every grownup needs the Word of God. Magdalena's brother, whom McGeary called Little Tim—because he couldn't pronounce the boy's indigenous name, was now ten years old, and he attended Henry's school religiously. But Magdalena didn't allow him to attend Henry's church services. The congregation's loud clapping and feverish praising frightened her. Therefore, she and Little Tim worshipped alone. At night, Magdalena knelt with him beside his bed with a string of rosary beads, and they said prayers to Jesus and Mary. Although McGeary respected his wife's spiritual practice, religion was not personally for him. He wanted nothing to interfere with his drinking and cigars.

Mr. Browski's wagon, too, continued coming into town the same as before. Magnolia had its own general store, and it was a popular, credit-extending shopping place. But Browski had a unique market angle, which was tough for the general store to compete with. He sold the finest and most expensive brands of everything from European silk lingerie to ivory-handled revolvers, and folks wanting something special eagerly came to him.

While so many things in Magnolia were changing, others stayed the same: the dust, the heat, the smoke from the mills; the fettered convicts out on lease, and the free men who worked the fields for a small salary. Ole Tom, at the end of his prison sentence, stayed around. McGeary appointed him guard over all his convict field-hands. There was no one better suited for maintaining security, for if a convict got out of hand, Ole Tom didn't hesitate to give them the lash.

36.

In 1886 life in Magnolia seemed tranquil, but it had simply withdrawn into itself, like a tide on a moonless night, appearing calm and quiet, but clashing beneath the surface with unseen forces. The first portent of events to come was an apparently innocuous sign, but one that was most unusual. McGeary had received numerous letters from Beatrice over the years, and he learned she had purchased a small hotel in Sacramento. She seemed to be doing well for herself, and each year she sent McGeary his portion of the profits along with a note of best wishes. Her words always beamed with gaiety and intelligence, much like Beatrice herself. Her most recent letter, though, was different in tone from all the others. Beatrice had married a man of local influence, and she believed she entered the ranks of the high-brows and socialites. But as fate would have it, her husband turned out to be a gambler and a womanizer. While Beatrice was willing to accept his womanizing as a defect common to most men, he was a poor gambler, and he squandered away every dollar she could earn. But that was not the full extent of his insidious behavior. Although Beatrice's letter made no explicit reference to it, McGeary read between its lines, and he realized her husband had a propensity for violence. It was obvious to McGeary that the man had given Beatrice a few thrashings.

The second portent happened weeks later when the warden stepped off the morning train. Instead of heading off toward the prison in his covered carriage, he mounted a horse to ride out to McGeary's. The captain was not at home, but Cassandra assured the warden that he would return within an hour. The warden waited on McGeary's porch, relaxing in a burnished rocker, graciously accepting Cassandra's offer of grapes and strawberries. When McGeary arrived, he stepped off his wagon and lifted a wood crate onto his shoulder.

Cassandra pushed the screen door open, and the two men passed through into the house. McGeary showed the warden the way into the kitchen, where, busting the crate open with his hands, he gave exposition to a bottle of French brandy. Breaking the paper seal on the bottle, he asked, "how 'bout a drink?"

"It's a bit early in the day for me," the warden replied. "I come out this way to have a talk." McGeary set the bottle aside and listened. "I was in the capital the last few days, making my disbursements," the warden said. "I had a meeting with a Federal official. The meeting was a serious matter. It seems the days of leasing convicts may soon be finished."

"The Federals finally did somethin', hu?" McGeary assumed. "What action they take?"

"None as yet," replied the warden. "But they will if we don't quit leasing convicts in South Fort County. I'll stall the Federals for as long as I can. But I won't be able to hold them off forever."

"You tell Madison and Fleshman yet?" asked McGeary.

"No, but I plan to."

"I'd like you to wait awhile."

"Why's that?"

"I'm thinkin' of makin' them a business proposition."

"What kind of business proposition?"

"The purchase of ten-thousand acres of Magnolia land."

"That's nearly half of all the land you own."

"It certainly is," McGeary agreed. "Every acre I have west of the Snake River. Three miles along its bank and four miles deep back to Eliot's old tract. Fleshman and Madison always wanted the best land in South Fort County. Maybe now they can have it."

"Without convict labor," the warden said. "The sugar business won't be very profitable. Cane land won't be worth what it is now. It's only fair I tell Fleshman and Madison about the Federals."

McGeary interpreted the warden's words as an unwillingness to cooperate. "I understand," said McGeary. "The conscience has a way of pullin' down on a man. If I had my druthers, I wouldn't do business with men like Fleshman and Madison. They're vipers. But if the opportunity presents itself, I'll put their money in my pocket same as I would at a poker table. It's the way the world turns 'round. I didn't start the world a spinnin'. I'm just along for the ride."

The warden rubbed his neck. "You certainly give a man something to think about," he said. "Funny though, I didn't hear you talk of loyalty. You're a man who respects loyalty, and I figured it to be foremost in your mind."

"I got no loyalty to Madison and Fleshman."

"I was referring to myself."

They two men lingered in the kitchen, questions waxing in their minds. The warden was the first to speak.

"How much cash per acre?"

"Oh, maybe fifty."

"That's about one-half-million dollars." The warden pondered the bountiful number. "And what's an acre worth without the benefit of convict labor?"

"Ten, maybe twelve dollars."

"Given the facts," the warden said. "I imagine it's possible for me to hold off on talkin' to Fleshman and Madison. For awhile anyway."

"I appreciate your cooperation. You'll be rewarded."

The warden walked alone to the door, but he stopped before crossing over its threshold. "Oh, I forgot to ask you. Do you remember my saying I met with a Federal official?"

"Yeah, of course I do."

"Well, you need to forget it."

McGeary's mind processed the warden's words. "I understand completely. You never mentioned a word."

37.

January 1887 was the windiest month anyone remembered. Browski's wagon rolled into Magnolia during the period to escape the big winds of the northern regions. His old body did not agree with the winter weather as was evident by his unrelenting coughs and sneezes. His illness, however, did not affect his doing business, for minutes after his arrival, he set up his wagon in a vacant space near the train depot and put out banners advertising his presence. McGeary's household members were Browski's best customers, and Magdalena, along with her mother and little Tim, paid him a visit.

"I got that fine white shawl you saw in the catalogue," Browski told Magdalena. "Special order." He handed her the item, and she placed it about her shoulders. Lifting its material to her face, she smelled its perfumed fabric. Brodski saw that she liked the shawl, but he was an adroit salesman, and he did not ask for immediate remittance. He instead began to show her other items to purchase. Reaching for a box in the corner of the wagon, his grasp was interrupted by a series of uncontrolled sneezes. When the seizures subsided, he opened the lid of the box and showed Magdalena a laced bonnet. "It comes all the way from Chicago," Browski said. "The very latest in ladies fashion." He encouraged her to try it on, but Magdalena's mother removed it from her daughter's hands. She then placed it on Little Tim's head, but she put it on backward, and it slipped down onto the bridge his nose. Magdalena and her mother laughed heartily, but not Browski. His laugh was weak, for robust laughter caused his lungs to expand, making them implode and causing Browski to cough violently.

"Are you sick, Mr. Browski?" asked Magdalena.

"Oh, no," he replied. "A tiny cold don't keep a good man down."

Magdalena's mother did not comprehend Browski's words, but she understood by his red eyes and runny nose that he was very ill. She nudged her daughter with her elbow, and she whispered that they should leave.

"How much for the shawl and the bonnet?" Magdalena asked Browski.

"Seventeen dollars," the vendor replied. "But for you, fifteen."

Magdalena pressed open the clip of her cash purse and handed Browski a few silver coins. "Thank you," she said politely.

Browski wiped his nose clean with the back of his hand. "Thank *you*," he whizzed. "I'll be around for a few more days. I hope to see you folks again."

Magdalena and her mother stepped away, and they began the short walk back to their carriage, Little Tim gaily skipping ahead.

That night, Magdalena awakened with a chill. She closed the windows of her bedroom and then went to check on her brother. She found him peacefully sleeping, but when she leaned over and kissed his cheek, she noticed his forehead was abnormally warm. She drew his blanket up over his tiny chest and made him snug. Returning to her room, she climbed into bed and fell fast asleep.

In the morning, she was abruptly wakened by the sounds of a hacking cough. Going into the hallway, she saw her father come up the stairs, a pot of hot tea in hand. They exchanged a few words in their indigenous language, and then he disappeared into his bedroom. Magdalena did not follow, but she continued on down the hall and entered the room of Little Tim. Both Bessie and Cassandra were at his bedside; Bessie held a cool, damp cloth to his forehead while Cassandra diligently watched from nearby.

"The boy be sick," Cassandra said the moment she noticed Magdalena enter the room. "The captain telegraphed the doctor in Junction, and he'll be here tomorrow—sometime before noon."

Magdalena stepped up to the bed, and she looked down at her brother. The strands of his black hair were wet with perspiration, and his eyes were shut to the light of the room. "Will he—be all right?" she asked, her concern evident by her stammer. "Is there something—I can do?"

"Ain't nothin' nobody can do," Bessie replied. She wrung out the cloth she used to cool Tim's head. "Only we gots to keep down the fever."

McGeary appeared in the doorway, and he peered at Little Tim with sympathetic eyes. Magdalena was the first to see the captain, and she rushed to him, embracing him like a frightened little girl. "Will he be okay?" she asked. "Will he?"

McGeary was touched, and he wanted to say a few consoling words. But the heat from Magdalena's face radiated onto his chest, and he realized that she too was sick with fever.

"It's best you rest," McGeary simply said.

"I'll be fine," Magdalena responded.

McGeary got Cassandra's attention, and he gestured for her to follow him out into the hallway. "The boy gonna be all right?" he asked.

"I can't say," the island woman replied. "We gonna have to wait on the doctor and see what he say."

"Can't you fix up some kind of potion?"

"Not when a boy got a fever like that. No telling about a potion. Sometime it got its own mind. Anything can happen."

Cassandra rejoined the other women in Little Tim's room. The boy closed his eyes, a tiny smile on his face. His breathing was soft, and Magdalena placed her head near his, her delicate hand resting upon his small chest. She also shut her eyes, and after awhile she fell into dreamy sleep.

Within the hour, Little Tim stopped breathing. His spirit passed quickly from this world into the next. And Magdalena, as if she had seen her brother pass over, followed him, and in another moment she also was dead.

There was wailing that day in the household, the likes of which McGeary had not heard since the war. And though he himself was rent asunder by anguish, he didn't shed a tear. He simply listened to the lamentations of his household and caressed the faces of those who found comfort in his arms.

38.

Ole Tom sat on his stallion with hawkish eyes overseeing three gangs of chained convicts. It was mid-afternoon, and Tom blew his whistle for the convicts to sit and to rest. Uniformed guards sat nearby, leaning back on their elbows in the cool ground. All was quiet, except for the occasional murmur of conversation. In the distance, a wagon crowded with free men came out of a low-lying field, and it climbed unto a dirt road that led to town. Another wagon appeared, and then another, all joining together in single file. A gang of convicts stood up, and they curiously watched the line of wagons as they wheeled along.

"Where they be goin'?" asked a convict.

"Ain't no concern of yers," Ole Tom replied.

"I knows, Mr. Tom," the convict responded humbly. "But I ain't never seen so many wagons of free men headin' to town."

"If you gotta know," Tom said crassly. "They gonna see McGeary bury his wife. She died of fever last night, the boy too."

"Holy Jesus," sighed the convict. "The captain's woman—she be dead."

The fettered men whispered among themselves, the news traveling hushed among their ranks. Ole Tom sounded his whistle and ordered the convicts back to work, but none obeyed. Instead, the convicts removed their hats from their heads, and some knelt down and prayed.

Ole Tom cracked his whip. "Git back to work!" he bellowed. The convicts, however, remained immobile. Tom raised his rifle, and he fired three shots into the air. "Git back to work or there be hell to pay!"

"We wants to pay our respects."

"You ain't free men! You're convicts!"

"All the same, Captain McGeary be good to us. He gonna give us a little place. Maybe a few acres."

"We takes care of the captain, and the captain takes care of us."

"That's right, Mr. Tom."

"We gots to show respects."

The convicts turned their eyes toward town, and the guards became unnerved. "What do we do, Tom?" a guard asked.

"Shoot the bastards!" Tom declared.

The guards touched their weapons, but it had little effect on the prisoners. The convicts took a step in the direction of town, their leg-irons nosily rattling.

"We can't shoot 'em all."

"The warden don't want us killin' convicts."

Ole Tom sat erect on his stallion, his small eyes squinting off into the distance, his mind considering his next move.

39.

The funeral procession rolled through a meadow, disturbing dandelion flowers and causing their seeds to float in the breeze. McGeary's wagon led the procession, and it carried the pine coffins of his wife and Little Tim. He traveled alone, preceded by a wagon driven by Magdalena's parents. Silas and Wilkie walked behind them, taking leaden, sober steps. The warden's carriage was at the rear of the procession, towed by a magnificent black colt of seventeen hands.

At the end of the meadow, the procession joined with the wagons of free men, and together they all moved up an embankment and onto a rise that overlooked the river where Andrew McGeary was interned seven years before. A pair of burial plots had been dug out that morning, and they lay open like wounds of the earth.

As the procession approached, the women of McGeary's household held hands and sang, tiny puffs of clouds above them seeming to listen to their choir. Once the coffins were set in the plots, Preacher Henry opened his Bible. All was quiet and unmoving, even the breeze, which paused as if to acknowledge the laws of God. Then sounds were heard, soft, faraway tolls that awakened the soul like the cords of a harp.

On the ridge across the river Ole Tom appeared. Sitting low in his saddle, he glanced over his shoulder, and he watched as a gang of convicts clamored over the ridge to join him. Within minutes, a throng of convicts numbering nearly one-hundred men filled the precipice of the hill. Once Henry felt that all was in order and settled in, he began the memorial service. The funeral ended within an hour, the convicts disappearing as swiftly as they arrived.

Afterward, McGeary sat in a rocker on the porch of his house, weighed in by heavy thoughts. He was flanked by Henry and the warden. Henry sat with his Bible tucked beneath his arm while the warden rested his eyes, his thumbs inserted in the straps of his suspenders.

Bessie appeared and breached the silence. "You best come, Captain. The girl's folks be fixin' to leave out tonight. They needs to wait, and I told 'em so, but they don't understand nothin' I says."

Henry offered to help. "I'll take care of this, Captain. I learned a few words of their language from Little Tim."

The warden waited for Henry to leave the left the porch, and then he began to speak. "I haven't heard anything more from the Federals, but for certain I will. You'll be the first to know. I imagine the Federals will give me orders on how to handle things. No telling what they'll say. I only hope there'll be enough time for you to consummate a deal with Fleshman and Madison."

McGeary sighed. "What will you do when it's all finished, Warden?"

"I don't know for sure. But I've been giving it some thought."

"What about the mines? You figure the Federals will soon shut them down?"

"Doubtful. The mines are owned by large corporations, mostly from up north. They've got big money to pass around, and they've also got political power. The Federals are shutting us down because our convicts work in the fields—in the light of day for everyone to see. The mines are different. Convicts work and live in the mines. No one sees them, and no one is the wiser." The warden stepped aboard his carriage. "It's getting late. I should be heading back. Let me know if I can help with anything."

McGeary stood, and crossing over to the carriage, he shook the warden's hand. "Thank you," he said warmly. "You're a good friend."

As the warden's carriage slipped away, the screen door of the house opened and Henry stepped forward onto the porch. "Magdalena's folks want to return home. They got a small place in the mountains. They're heavy with grief, and no one can change their minds. I convinced them to wait until morning. I imagine they'll leave out early."

The next morning McGeary waited for Magdalena's folks to come out of the house. It was before dawn, but the sky was orange on the eastern horizon, and in the west a blue, waning moon was setting down. Magdalena's parents exited the house, carrying their personal items, which were rolled up inside blankets and bound with rope. McGeary helped the old folks aboard his wagon, and he taxied them to the train depot.

It was an hour before the train was scheduled to arrive. McGeary stepped inside the office and purchased a pair of tickets. He handed the tickets to his in-laws, and then he reached inside his trousers pockets. Withdrawing two sacks of coins, he placed them in the care of Magdalena's father. He weighed them with his hands, and looking inside he saw the coins were gold. He hid the sacks away in his pack, and Magdalena's mother tearfully embraced McGeary. When the train arrived, they stepped aboard, and waving goodbye one last time, they were content to depart the land of cane.

40.

A month passed before a deal with Fleshman and Madison was consummated. McGeary had waited until they offered forty-five dollars an acre. Figuring they had reached their limit, he finally agreed to sell. Once McGeary had the warden's cash in hand, he sent Silas out to the prison to tell him to come to the train deport the following day. The warden arrived at noon, and making an inquiry into McGeary's whereabouts, a man directed him to a warehouse where McGeary kept a crude, but airy office.

"Congratulations," the warden told the captain. "I hope you got the price you wanted."

"Yeah, and a little more," said McGeary. "I've got a somethin' for you too." McGeary set his attention on a bill of lading atop his desk. Unable to accurately discern its contents, he donned a pair of wire-rimmed eye glasses and quietly proceeded to decipher it.

The warden's concern, however, was related to cash. "Did you bring it, Captain?" he asked.

"Oh, yeah," the captain replied, remaining focused on the bill of lading. "The six crates behind me. Wilkie James will help you load 'em on your wagon."

"I came on horseback," the warden explained, his thumbs pulling on his suspenders. "I didn't know my loyalty would be rewarded by six cases whiskey."

McGeary peered up over the rims of his spectacles and gazed quixotically at the warden "Is that what you think it is?" he asked with a grin.

The warden inspected a crate. Opening it, he affirmed its contents. "Looks to be whiskey to me," he said. Flustered, he shuffled about like a cock with ruffled feathers.

McGeary was in good humor, and he played the warden along. "Take out a bottle," he suggested. "Let's have a drink. It's damn good Scotch Whiskey."

"I don't drink until the damned evening," said the warden quick as a bullet.

"That's a shame," McGeary responded. "But you can pour me a drink, can't you? I don't like to wait 'til evenin'."

Burdened with disgust, the warden lifted out a bottle from its box. "Baby Jesus!" he abruptly cried out. Then, lifting out another, he stared at the floor of the crate. "How much cash is there?" the warden asked, astonished by what he saw.

"Ten thousand maybe," McGeary replied. "I don't much care for countin' out cash. The six crates should add up to fifty thousand."

"Fifty-thousand dollars!" roared the warden. "This is just too much, Captain. I never imagined—"

"You can give it back," said McGeary comically. "I'll accept it— no hard feelings—I'll understand. Some men want to have a clear conscience."

The warden reached down inside the crate and grasped a bundle of cash. "Like I said before, Captain, you're the damnedest fella I ever met." He fanned the cash across his face. "Tell me, why did you put it at the bottom of these crates of whiskey?"

"It seemed like a safe place," McGeary answered. "But we can stuff it into a burlap bag if you want. Anyways, the whiskey is yours." McGeary stepped out of his office and summoned Wilkie. "Draw up a wagon," he instructed. "And load the whiskey crates. Ride out to the prison with the warden, and see he gets there safe."

"Yes, Captain," Wilkie responded.

The warden walked outdoors with McGeary into the open air. "Thanks for the fifty-thousand" he said, in a genuinely heart-felt way.

"No need to say thanks," said McGeary. "Like I say, you earned it."

The warden secured his horse to the rear of the wagon, and then he climbed aboard the drivers seat. McGeary, though, folded his arms across his chest, and he gazed thoughtfully toward the sky.

"Something on your mind, Captain?" the warden asked. Removing his Winchester from its sheath, he set it behind his seat. "I'll be fine getting back."

"I'm sure you will," McGeary said. "But I was just wonderin'—what'll happen to the convicts when you close the prison?"

"The real bad ones will be transferred to other facilities," the warden replied. "The others I'll have to set free. Some will likely want to stay and work the fields. The others will find a way back home."

"Those who wants to stay on can see Silas or Wilkie. I'll give 'em work and make sure they're paid fairly. Tell the others that a train ticket waits for 'em at the depot. They'll also get five dollars. That way they won't go home broke."

"You're a generous man," said the warden. "Not many men are like you."

"It all comes down to business," McGeary explained. "The town needs men who wanna work—to earn more profit it's gotta grow."

"Folks are going call it a Negro town," the warden opined.

"No," McGeary corrected. "Folks are gonna call it *Sugarville*."

41.

The prison was quiet when the warden got back. The convicts had yet to return from the fields. Many of the guards rested in their barracks, and only a few men were on duty— the lieutenant and a squad of sentries atop the wall. Wilkie removed the whiskey crates from the wagon and set them inside a heavily secured office.

"You be needin' me anymore, Warden?" asked Wilkie.

"No, that'll be all," the warden replied.

Wilkie exited the office, but he stood outside the door, watching and listening, remembering the days when he was in prison.

The warden noticed Wilkie and approached him. "Not many men return to this place. You must have some awful memories. Being here now brings back those memories. It's best you head on."

Wilkie, however, didn't leave. "I don't never recall it being so quiet like this," he said. "There was always the sounds of chains— even at night when ever'body was sleepin'. Some of us down-low used to toss and turn', havin' terrible dreams and such." Wilkie's voice was melancholy, and it enraptured the warden. "You hear that, Warden?" Wilkie asked. "It's them down-low—some be singin' out, and others be cryin' for The Lord."

The warden was baffled, for he heard nothing. "I don't hear anything," he said.

"I knows, Warden," Wilkie responded. "Some men hears, and others don't."

Wilkie boarded the wagon and headed toward home, leaving the warden standing alone in the prison yard. The warden watched Wilkie as he passed through the gate, wondering why Wilkie had not spoken bitterly of his days in prison. He wished that he had, for the warden had a crusty edge, and he could easily fend off bitter words. But as it were, Wilkie's voice cut through the warden's defenses and awakened things inside him—goodly things that had long laid dormant; things that are born unto the soul of a child, yet are lost when the child becomes a man.

The warden returned inside the office. Removing the stacks of cash from the bottom of the crates, he placed them in an iron safe behind a rack of rifles.

The lieutenant entered and offered his services. "Need some help, Warden?"

"Yeah, bring up the convicts from down-low. Take them over to the pump and let them bathe. Give them something proper to eat."

"You want them to clean up down-low? It's stinking something awful."

"No, when the convicts come in from the fields, have a gang fill it in with dirt."

The lieutenant's instincts told him to object. "Are you sure that's what you want to do? It may not be the best thing."

The warden's eyes instantly glinted with wrath. "Are you questioning my orders?"

"No, Warden. I only sought clarification."

The warden regained his poise. "I understand. You're a good man. I've got a few crates of whiskey inside the office. Take a couple of them to the guard's barracks. Keep a crate for yourself."

The lieutenant snapped to attention. "Yes sir! I'll take care of that."

When the convicts came in from the fields, the lieutenant unshackled a gang of men, and he directed them to fill in the hole that was known as down-low. All the other convicts watched with intense eyes, listening to the clangs of shovels, watching as down-low disappeared under a cover of dust and dirt.

42.

Spring came late in Magnolia in 1887. It was nearly May before green leaves budded on branches, and blue jays sang with the starlings. Convicts in the fields worked warmly planting stalks of cane; by slow degrees, hundreds of stubbles filled the lines of furrows, waiting for the days of big sun and heavy rain.

The warden hadn't told anyone about the imminent closing of the prison, and when he finally did, those affected by the closure were astounded, especially the convicts. He informed them on a Saturday, a day when the convicts labored only until noon. He gathered the populace together after they had their afternoon meal. From a sentry post atop the wall, he hollered down to them in clear tones.

"The Federals have ordered me to shut down South Fort Prison. Most of you convicts will be set free, your sentences lawfully commuted, and all your fines forgiven. Those of you who want to return home can pick up a train ticket at the depot in Magnolia. You'll also receive five dollars in silver coin. Some of you might want to stay and work in McGeary's fields. Speak to Silas or Wilkie James, and they'll find you work at a decent wage." The lieutenant of the guards stood nearby, and the warden called him to his side. "We'll release two-hundred convicts within the hour," he told his second-in-command. "They'll have plenty of time to board the afternoon train. Tomorrow we'll set others free. The rest we'll release on Monday. In the meantime, pass around the new shirts and overalls that came in last week. Take away the convict's old prison clothes and burn them outside the gate."

"Yes sir, Warden."

"Come by my office when you have the time. I've got cash bonuses for you and the other men."

When the first gangs of convicts were unshackled, they meandered about in the prison yard like lost cattle in search of water. But soon they found their bearings, and passing through the prison gate, they heading off into freedom. By noon the following Monday, every convicts had left the prison. Five-hundred and seventy souls elected to return to their homes while two-hundred and fifty decided to remain in Magnolia.

43.

When word reached Fleshman and Madison informing them that their convicts had not come out to work the fields, they went directly to the prison. It was a curious sight, for the gate was ajar, and the guards who usually manned the wall were conspicuously gone.

"What the hell is going on, Warden?" Fleshman asked the warden, the moment he and Madison entered his office.

"Concerning what?" the warden asked.

"Concerning our God-damned convicts!" Fleshman cried out.

Madison motioned for Fleshman to remain calm. "Our fields are idle," he told the warden. "And we're wondering why the prison gate is open. The question upper-most in our minds is, where's all your prisoners?"

"I don't rightly know," the warden replied. "On their way home, I imagine." Before either Fleshman or Madison could utter a word, the warden passed them a telegram. "As you can see, the United States Attorney General has ordered the closure of the South Fort Penal Facility. I had no choice but to release the convicts. The few murders and robbers we had I sent upstate to another facility. The prisoners who had fines to pay, I let them walk away."

"Hundreds of convicts just walk off into the sunset?"

"Pretty much."

"Why didn't you tell us about this earlier?"

"Well, you can see the telegram is dated the day before yesterday. I didn't have a chance to get out your way. Besides, I figured you'd come see me when the convicts didn't show up. And here you are."

Fleshman examined the telegram, then angrily crumbled it with his fist and tossed it onto the floor. "You've known about this for months. There were rumors in the capital about this, but everyone thought it was just that—rumors. You waited until we bought McGeary's land for nearly fifty dollars an acre. That land now is worth only ten."

"What do you have to say for yourself?" asked Madison.

"Nothing for myself," the warden replied. "But for you gentlemen, I'll say that leasing convicts is a dangerous business. High profit means high risk."

Fleshman exploded. "You self-righteous son-of-a-bitch! Don't talk to us like we just fell off the melon wagon. We're not some kids you're messing with. We've got investors in the capital. When they find out how much cash you've cost them, they'll hang you from the nearest tree." Fleshman flushed with red. "Maybe we should save them the trouble. We've got a dozen armed men on the other side of the river."

Madison spoke with a cooler head. "It's a simple matter of business," he explained. "One-half-million dollars is an awful lot of money. Unfortunately, someone will have to pay. So, unless you've got a few hundred thousand in cash on hand, you'll have to pay in some other manner."

The warden let out a long, winded sigh. "I hear your message loud and clear. I certainly don't want to get hurt over something like this. I imagine I can come up with sufficient cash to cover a good portion of the losses. I've been at this business for more than a decade, and I've been smart enough to sock away a good bit of cash."

Fleshman grinned, a sardonic, satisfactory grin. Madison, a man of a higher class, simply nodded his approval.

The warden stepped over to his open window, and he shouted down below. "Lieutenant, come up here!"

Once the lieutenant arrived, he crossed the room and stood at attention. "Reporting as ordered, sir."

"What are you packing?" the warden asked him.

"Well, nothing," the lieutenant replied uncomfortably "The prisoners are gone. I didn't think that—"

The prison boss didn't allow the officer to complete his thought. "It's okay," said the warden, reaching into a drawer of his desk. He withdrew a 45-caliber revolver and handed it over. "Take this," he instructed.

The lieutenant accepted the weapon and held it in his hands, wondering what to do with it.

"Press its barrel to that man's neck," the warden instructed. The lieutenant obeyed, and lowering his weapon, he pointed it at Fleshman. "Now, count down twenty seconds. If he's still in my office when you get to zero, put a bullet in his throat. Then put a bullet in this other man here. We don't want any witnesses."

"Any particular place I should shoot this other one?" the lieutenant asked.

"Wherever you can," the warden answered. "He'll likely be running for the door, and it's tough to drop a moving target."

"You're making it more difficult for yourself," Madison announced.

The warden disregarded his words, and he gave the lieutenant further instructions.

"Once you shoot the two of them, drag them over to the window and toss them out. Go down into the yard and load them onto a wagon. Take them out to where we buried the last few convicts. Make sure their bodies are never found."

"You're bluffing!" Fleshman expounded. "You won't murder two men in your own office."

"Well, I don't recall having any visitors today," the warden answered.

Then the lieutenant began the countdown. "Twenty, nineteen, eighteen, seventeen—" He interrupted himself. "Warden, you should clear your desk of any important papers. They won't look right stained with blood."

"Oh, you're right," said the warden. Promptly gathering up the papers on his desk, he shut them away in a drawer.

"And step back a few a few paces," the lieutenant suggested. "You know a 45-caliber makes a man splatter something awful."

"Perhaps I should just step out of the office," the warden said.

"That would be best," the lieutenant agreed.

Fleshman jumped out of his chair, and he stomped toward the door. "We'll be back! And we'll bring armed men with us."

"You do that," the warden retorted. "I've got thirty armed guards in the barracks, and a warehouse full of weapons and shells. So you come on by. We'll have a shootout."

"We have the cannon as well, sir," the lieutenant reminded the warden.

"Yeah, that's right," the warden mused. "We got a cannon."

44.

Within the week, most of the arms and munitions owned by the state was moved out of the facility, and shipped off to the capital, many of the prison's guards accompanying the small citadel. The warden, along with six of his most trusted men, stayed behind, making final arrangement for the wagons and animals. On Sunday, when all the arrangements were complete, the facility was vacated, and they occupied the prison for the final time. The group left out together. The lieutenant rode with the warden in his covered carriage led by the princely colt. The other guards followed the carriage in an open wagon, the cannon rolling behind them on squeaking wheels.

The squad went directly to McGeary's place, and they found the captain outdoors sitting at a picnic table drinking a cup of coffee.

McGeary surveyed the heavily armed column. "Looking to start a war somewhere?"

The warden beamed proudly, "No, but if one breaks out, we're ready."

The comment amused the guards and they chuckled. The lieutenant stepped off the warden's carriage and climbed aboard the wagon.

The warden gestured to McGeary, indicating that he should join him. "Ride with me to the depot. I've something I want to give you."

McGeary pulled himself aboard the carriage, and it slowly trekked off.

"So our business is finally done," McGeary commented once they had gotten down the road.

"Pretty much," said the warden.

"Thought any more about what you'll do now?"

"Yeah, I'll head back home. I've a got a daughter and a son-in-law. He's a bright fellow, and he's got some business ideas. Hell, maybe I'll earn a fortune. Thanks to you I can give it a try. St. Louis has opportunities."

"St. Louis? I didn't figure you for a city boy."

"Actually I'm not. I grew up in a town about thirty miles out. It's called Potterstown."

"Yeah, I heard of it."

"Town's got only fifty citizens. How'd you hear about the place?"

"During the war I passed through that way."

"That's right. You were an officer for the confederacy. I was an officer too. But for the union."

"Where'd you see action?"

"I didn't. I commanded a facility for captured confederate soldiers. The only action I recall concerns Colonel Robley. We had him for awhile—until his raiders managed to bust him out."

"The bloody colonel is nobody to have around," McGeary commented.

The warden peered curiously at McGeary. "The only ones to call him *the bloody colonel* were his own raiders," he said.

McGeary leaned forward and rested his arms on his knees. "I rode with him for a year," he began. "Ain't nothin' I'm proud of doin'. I was young and wild, and wicked too. Then one day I came to my senses. I left the raiders, and I joined the regulars out of Virginia. They made me a captain 'cause I rode with Robley. By this time, though, the fight had gone out of me. I kept my men safe and out of conflict when possible. It gave me a reputation different from the one I had with the raiders." McGeary stretched back and stroked his beard. "Strange, ain't it? One day I'm a vicious killer, and they call me a hero. Then the next day I'm keepin' men from needlessly dyin', and they call me a coward."

"The world is quite a paradox."

"Yeah, whatever you call it, I've had my share of it."

The guards unloaded the wagon and unhitched the cannon, moving all their possessions onto the platform of the depot. Taking posts as sentries, the guards looked down the roads of town, keeping watch for anything suspicious. The blare of the train whistle sounded in the distance, and the warden firmly shook hands with McGeary.

"Someone from the stable will come by to pick up the wagon," the warden explained. "I'd like for you to take care of my carriage and the horse. It's the best animal in the county, maybe in the whole damn state."

"When are you comin' back?" McGeary asked.

"I've no plans to return," replied the warden.

"Then what do I do with the horse and the carriage?"

"Ride them, I imagine."

McGeary admired the handsome colt. "I don't get many gifts from folks. So I kinda don't know what to say."

The warden smiled and shook his head whimsically. "Like I always said, you're the damnedest fella I ever met."

45.

In early July of the year, McGeary decided to take a vacation into the Sierra Madres in New Mexico Territory. He intended his journey to be more than an opportunity to get away for awhile, but also to give those nearest him a chance to move on—to make a new life elsewhere.

Cassandra decided to return to her island. McGeary gave her sufficient cash for the journey, and if she were frugal, it would keep her comfortable for the rest of her life. Bessie and Wilkie James wished to remain in Magnolia and to continue working for McGeary. Satisfied with their decision, McGeary promised to set aside a hundred acres of land for them, and to build them a sizeable home.

Silas was something altogether different.

McGeary invited Silas to join him for Sunday breakfast, and mid-way through the meal he conveyed his feelings. "You been with me goin' on more than ten years," he began. "You been loyal, and I'm a man who respects that. There ain't many ways to compensate loyalty, except perhaps with cash." McGeary laid his hand on an envelope atop the table, and he pushed it toward Silas. "There's enough cash here to get you started somewhere, to make a good life for yourself. No sense staying in Magnolia. There's better places to live than here."

Silas opened the envelope and looked inside. "I never seen so much cash," he said. "How much you figure is here, Captain?"

"Ten-thousand dollars," McGeary replied. "There's more if you need it."

Silas lapsed into sober thought. "If it's all the same to you, Captain," he said, pushing the envelope back across the table. "I'll be staying on here. I got no place to go. My baby girl Mabel be married now and living back home with her fella. Young folks don't want an old man around. They gots they own minds about doin' things."

"What will you do in Magnolia?" asked McGeary.

"Stay on with you, Captain," Silas replied indignantly. "I gots work to do here. Somebody have to do the fixin' of things. Wagons wheels gettin' busted all the time. And that colt the warden give you, somebody gots to look after him. That animal be no field horse. He be somethin' special."

"I agree with that," said McGeary. "If you wanna stay, it's fine by me. You've always been like family. About the cash, though, it's yours. Stay or leave."

McGeary nudged the envelope closer to Silas.

"I won't know to do with so much cash," said Silas. "I gots to think 'bout it some." He paused thoughtfully, and moving his eyes across the ceiling, he came to a decision. "I can send some to Mabel. Young folks like spending of money. They might could buy a house—and not no shanty, but a big place with a porch along the sides."

"That right," McGeary agreed. "They can do that."

"And I seen some fancy clothes at the general store," Silas went on. "I always been wantin' fancy clothes, and a high hat like rich folks wear. Yeah, I be sendin' some cash to Mabel, and I be gettin' me some fancy clothes."

46.

Making plans to depart later in the month, McGeary asked Silas to accompany him and to leave his responsibilities in the hands of others for awhile. Silas was at first reluctant, but he soon agreed, saying he'd never seen mountains before, and the trip would be an opportunity to show off his new outfit.

The two men boarded the Mid-West Southern, traveling north for two days. Then they headed west into New Mexico Territory. When the train climbed into the Sierra Madres, the peaks were capped with snow. The hills below were brushed with evergreens, and their slopes were laced with amber-colored roads.

"Where we headin' Captain?" Silas asked.

"Santa Fe," replied McGeary. "I passed through the town years ago. Lots of poker playin' and drinkin' tequila. Like most any town, it's got some good folks, but it's also got some bad. We'll stay a few days, and then head north into Colorado."

The rail station in Santa Fe was located two streets from *la alameda,* a square-block park in the center of town. Along the park's perimeters were small government offices built of adobe, each mingling among open-air shops and lively patio restaurants. Inside *la alameda,* potted flora decorated stone pathways; sleepy-eyed guitarists in sombreros played songs for a few centavos, and vendors with pushcarts sold roasted ears of corn.

At the main entrance to the park, an elegant woman in a flowered hat negotiated the sale of a turquoise bracelet with a Navaho girl. She held the item up to the rays of the sun, admiring its polished blue stones. A hired carriage carrying McGeary and Silas passed by, and Silas, believing he recognized the lady in the flowered hat, thrust his head out the window and gawked at her.

Silas bounced back onto his seat, excited by what he saw. "I just seen Miz Beatrice!" he proclaimed.

"Don't be foolish," McGeary snapped. "She's a thousand miles west of here in Sacramento."

"I gots to see for myself," Silas asserted.

Suffering the whims of his companion, McGeary signaled the driver to stop the carriage. Silas merrily hopped out and hurried toward the woman. Approaching her from behind, he politely tapped her on the shoulder. The lady disregarded it, for she judged the action improper. Parading off toward a crowd of passersby, she hoped to disappear. But before she was able to do so, Silas called out in a lurid voice. "Miz Beatrice!"

The lady pivoted, and searching out the source of the voice, her eyes landed on Silas. She stepped toward him, her mind flashing with wonderment.

"Oh my, I simply cannot believe it!"

"I knowed it was you, Miz Beatrice. The captain says I talks like a fool. But wait 'til he sees."

"Addison is here?"

"He be in the carriage."

Beatrice bustled over to the carriage, and finding the covering of the window drawn down, she swung the door open. "Addison, what are you doing here?" she asked delightfully.

McGeary levered himself up from his seat, and he lugged his body through the small carriage door. He reached forward and tenderly touched Beatrice's face. "I imagine I could ask you the same."

"I'm on my way to Magnolia—to see you. I wrote you a letter. Didn't you receive it?"

"No. But it don't much matter now. Silas and me come up this way to see the mountains. We're just gettin' into town."

"Then you simply *must* stay at my hotel. It's the best in Santa Fe, but I'm afraid it won't much impress you."

"We're not lookin' for much—just a place where we can rest."

"Got to rest up when travelin'," Silas added. "Two days ride by train makes a fella tired—and hungry too."

"Wonderful," said Beatrice. "I'll help you get settled in. And Addison, I have something to give you."

"I don't need a gift," McGeary said shyly.

"It's not a gift," Beatrice responded. "It's your share of the profits from our business."

McGeary was pleased, and taking Beatrice by the hand, he helped her into the carriage.

The Hotel *La Hacienda* had little to brag about. The courtyard's floor was cracked and patched with mud tiles. The columns supporting its archway leaned a few degrees, and beams of wood above were warped and rotten. However, the hotel lobby vastly contrasted the courtyard. The front desk was made of mahogany and craved by artisans. The dome ceiling overhead had a facade of colorful titles, and a brass chandelier hung down. It glowed in an old-world motif, illuminating the lobby's wood and ceramic floor.

"So much has happened this year," Beatrice said as they waited for the desk clerk to attend to them. "My husband died suddenly last spring."

"How did it happen?" McGeary asked.

"It was a tragic accident," Beatrice replied. "He fell from a horse. There wasn't much the doctors could do."

Beatrice sadly hung her head, but McGeary detected that it was disingenuous.

The desk clerk suddenly appeared.

Beatrice made the arrangements. "My friends require accommodations," she said. "And kindly give me my envelope."

The desk clerk opened a strong box below the desk, and he lifted out a sealed envelope. Beatrice received the envelope from the clerk, and she passed it to McGeary who, without so much as a cursory inspection, tucked it in his coat pocket.

"Don't you want to know how much it is, Addison?"

"It can't be too much."

"You're right. I'm sorry it's not more."

Shortly thereafter, McGeary and Silas unpacked their baggage. When they finished they lay down on the bed, McGeary positioned on one side, and Silas at the other. McGeary shut his eyes without sleeping.

"Why you puts us in one room?" Silas asked. "I don't much mind. It be fine with me. But ever since we seen Miz. Beatrice, you been actin' strange. I mean no offence, Captain. But you's the kind of man who stays to hissself."

McGeary didn't bother to sit up to respond to Silas. "Seein' Miz Beatrice has changed things. I don't exactly know what happened in Sacramento, but I know it weren't good." He rolled over onto one side and looked over at his companion. "I'm asking you not to talk 'bout my cane business with Beatrice. I've prospered over the years, but she don't need to know that."

"I understands, Captain."

"Maybe, maybe not. But there's a lot more to this than meets the eye."

"Well, I knows money can change folks—make 'em do things—sometimes bad things."

"I don't look to judge Beatrice. But dealin' with her is the same as doin' business. It's best not to show your hand." McGeary rolled back over, and he shut his eyes once more. "Let's get some sleep. We'll all soon have a good meal together."

47.

Beatrice watched as McGeary came down the hotel stairs. He wore a suede jacket, a white shirt, and a western string-tie. Silas followed behind him, but he was attired far more debonair. He wore a black tuxedo with tails, a top hat, and polished leather boots. Toting a staff, he stylishly descended the stairs, his broad chest expanded and his head held high.

Beatrice was so impressed by Silas that she took him by the arm and sauntered with him into the dining room. "You look absolutely exquisite," she said. "My how things must have changed in Magnolia!"

"No, it still be a bowl of dust," responded Silas. "I been savin', my wages for goin' on ten years, and I bought me these fancy clothes. I seen pictures in magazines. Folks say they's *butlers* clothes. Other times folks say they's clothes of *valets*."

Beatrice smiled, endeared to Silas. "And you'd like to be Addison's valet?" she asked sweetly.

"Oh, I already be the captain's valet—that is after I finish with the heavy chores."

McGeary pulled a chair away from a table in the corner of the dining room, and he helped Beatrice to sit. Getting comfortable with a bottle of wine, they ordered dinner. The captain requested a double portion of *chuletas ahumada*, smoked pork steak, along with a plate of refried beans and Spanish rice. Silas ordered *caldo de res,* a rich broth of boiled beef, squash, potatoes, corn and cabbage. Beatrice asked for a modest meal, *Sopa Azteca,* which is a tomato broth with sheds of chicken breast, topped off with goat cheese, and thin strips of tortilla chips.

"Where you be headin' to, Miz Beatrice?" Silas asked. "St. Louis?"

"New Orleans," Beatrice replied. "I plan to board a vessel to France."

"Should be nice to visit family," said McGeary. "It's been many years."

"Yes, I'm so excited," Beatrice said. "My dear niece is engaged to the son of an English Baron. The wedding will be next spring. She wants me to visit her, and she's promised to introduce me in the Queen's Court." Beatrice swelled with pride. "Imagine me in the Queen's Court!" She suddenly softened hr voice. "Perhaps I'll meet a handsome Baron—an old, wealthy one."

The conversation at the table was deafened by voices of rowdy men at the bar. A group of vaqueros and gunslingers made rude comments, and they taunted the few gentlemen who drank liquor nearby. McGeary tried to ignore them, but the racket increased, and the men became more audacious.

"Look at the dude!" shouted one of the men. "I never seen a Negro dressed so pretty."

"He must be a rich fella," said another man. "Made a fortune pickin' cotton!"

Their comments rankled McGeary, and he shoved back from the table and stood up.

"Don't bother with them," said Beatrice. "They're drunk and talking foolish."

"I'm gettin' a drink," said McGeary. "I'll be fine."

"Captain, ain't no need," said Silas. "I gots to get some rest, and be goin' on upstairs."

Silas departed quietly, leaving his companions alone.

"Please, Addison," Beatrice begged. "Those men only want trouble."

The Captain signaled for the waiter. "Beatrice, wait for me in the courtyard," he said. "I'll pay for the meal, and then I'll be along." He stepped away from the table, and he gave the waiter a few gold coins. "That's for the meal, and drinks for the men at the bar. But tell 'em next time they're rude to my friend, I'll bust their skulls open."

48.

In the morning the trio of friends departed Santa Fe and headed north into Colorado. The single-coach train trekked sluggishly as it wound around mountains and over trestles. It paused at towns and villages, and Beatrice visited with vendors of turquoise and tiny trinkets. Silas found turquoise curious, for he had never seen polished blue stones. He examined a ring, and he slipped it on his index finger. Its large, oval stone was set in silver, and it appeared to be costly.

"It's reasonably priced," Beatrice explained. "The Navaho are wonderful craftsman. In Europe such jewelry costs so much more."

Silas tendered a few coins for the ring. McGeary watched the exchange from the patio of a restaurant nearby.

Silas showed McGeary his purchase, his eyes proudly alight with ownership. "I buys it with my own wages," he said.

"It's a fine piece," said the captain. "Fine enough for a gentleman."

"Addison, let's go for a walk," Beatrice suggested. "There's a crest west of town that overlooks a beautiful valley."

McGeary looked to Silas. "Care to join us?" he asked.

"No, Captain," Silas replied. "I'll sit here awhile. Have me a brandy, and a smoke."

Beatriced laughed in feminine fashion. "You certainly *are* a gentleman," she said. "You enjoy the good things in life."

"Yes, Miz Beatrice," responded Silas. "I be tryin' my best."

It was a twenty-minute walk to the hilltop crest, and it looked out over a magnificent valley. Beatrice was so impressed by the panorama that it caused her to longingly moan.

"Oh, it's so lovely—perhaps the most gorgeous place on earth."

Miles beyond the valley a line of jagged mountains laid in magnificent solace. A river meandered down along the mountainsides, and after countless windings and turns, it flowed into the valley below, passing a ranch house that was barely discernable among a section of evergreens.

"My goodness—it's such a beautiful home. The family there must be so happy. However, it's so remote—miles from anywhere. I don't believe I could live in such a place. But it would be a nice home to vacation in. It's little more than a cabin actually."

Actually, it was much more than a cabin, but in the far distance it appeared small to Beatrice. It was a lavish ranch house larger than any abode in South Fort County, and beyond the ranch house, where the hills sloped down into a grand valley, cattle roamed over six-thousand acres of grazing land.

"Why not purchase a little place like that?" Beatrice asked McGeary. "It wouldn't cost much, and it would a nice escape from the hot summers in Magnolia."

"The cane business ain't been so good," McGeary replied. "Now that the leasing of convicts is done, there's little money to be made. I got a comfortable life, but I ain't a rich man."

"I'm sorry," said Beatrice. "I didn't know."

McGeary had no regret about misleading Beatrice, for though he believed she was a good woman, he also knew she had clever designs.

"Let's get back to the village," said McGeary. "Continue travelin' up north—Colorado's a big place. Towns are growin' up everywhere."

When the pair got back to town they found Silas napping in a wicker chair outside a shop that sold wool blankets and ponchos. He wakened when his friends approached.

"I had me a dream, Captain," he said. "Like no dream I had before." He stood up wearily, but there was a twinkle in his eye. "You, and me, and Miz Beatrice, we was walkin'. on the clouds. They was cool, and soft. We was driftin' this way and that way. It felt like we was in heaven. Maybe heaven be like a dream. Maybe my dream be from heaven."

.

49.

McGeary found one town to his liking, a bustling municipality of ranchers and miners—a place where some earned fortunes and others hard luck. The town's biggest hotel was situated at a high point that provided scenic views of sunsets, which always glowed with red and amber. Beatrice and McGeary stayed together in a large room while Silas stayed in a smaller room nearby. The large room had a terrace, and each evening Beatrice went out onto it where she looked out at Mother Nature.

"Addison, it's wonderful in the Sierra Madres," she said early one evening. The vespers of night had not begun to fall, and the atmosphere was exceedingly fair. "Look, there's a river—high in the mountains. I never noticed it before."

McGeary surveyed the heights of the faraway hills, and he saw a gap that broke through the summit of the peaks. "In the spring the snow will melt," he explained. "The river will deepen and run down to the valley. It's the source of the Snake River."

"The Snake River—the same as in Magnolia?" Beatrice asked. "My goodness, it's difficult to believe. The water that flows from the grandeur of heaven also flows into a hell hole."

McGeary had disdain for her declaration. "A hell hole," he echoed edgily. "Well, it's what some folks say."

"I'm sorry, Addison," said Beatrice, recognizing her blunder. "Magnolia is your home. I shouldn't have spoken so harshly."

"No, you shouldn't," said McGeary. "But the truth is back home don't much compare with Colorado."

Beatrice became pensive. "How odd," she said, ruminating. "Something has always puzzled me. Years ago when I departed Magnolia, I looked back at the land, and it appeared so lovely. I've never understood how the land could have seemed so different." She took McGeary's hand, and she peered softly into his eyes. "I wonder how things would be—if I had stayed in Magnolia and not gone to California. I left because I hoped to find a better life." Beatrice stepped away from McGeary, and she fell back onto the bed. "I didn't find what I wanted. I only found regrets."

"What's done is done," said McGeary. "There's no changin' the past. But the future is somethin' different. We can change the future."

"Oh, Addision," Beatrice said, her emotions bringing her close to tears. "I don't want to make any more mistakes. I want to be happy." She rallied her sentiments and spoke more bravely. "I know I seem happy. I speak joyfully, and I act so content. But I'm not. I'm not happy at all, and I wonder if I ever will be."

McGeary saw it was time to speak what was on his mind ever since he saw Beatrice in Santa Fe. "Maybe I got no right to ask," he began. "I'm not a rich man, and Magnolia is no place for an elegant woman. But one day things can be better. Maybe cane will become more profitable."

Beatrice sat up on the edge of the bed. "Addison, I owe you much," he said. "But returning to Magnolia, well, it's something I would have to think about."

Beatrice stood, and she paced the room.

McGeary watched as she paced back and forth. "There's plenty time to decide," McGeary assured her. "I'll wait."

Beatrice needed only a few moments. "No, I've already decided," she said resolutely. "I'll go with you to Magnolia. I know it's unbearably hot at times. Perhaps we can visit Colorado for a few weeks each summer—that is if we have some extra cash. Whatever should happen, I'll not complain. I'll be happy. I promise."

"What about goin' to Europe?" McGeary asked. "Don't you wanna marry an English baron?"

Beatrice pressed her warm lips to McGeary's cheek, and she kissed him. "With my luck, he'd be a charlatan," she replied.

They both smiled, and then they began to laugh—warm, ironic, endearing laughter.

The three companions remained another week in Colorado and then returned to Santa Fe. Before McGeary departed on the train he secretly made arrangements to purchase a ranch with two-thousand acres. He agreed to pay thirty-five-thousand dollars for it, and he didn't bother to negotiate. He knew what he had, and not merely for the richness of the land, but for a river that flowed from the heights of the mountains, winding over the earth for hundreds of miles, and then slithering into the lowlands.

EPILOGUE

Beatrice and McGeary remained together, living a prosperous life unto old age. They dwelled in Sugarville during winter, spring and autumn, and then vacationed each summer at their ranch in the mountains of Colorado. McGeary died in 1908, leaving a large portion of his estate to the town as well as to those who for years had worked loyally for him. He was buried on the hill that overlooks Snake River alongside the graves of Andrew, Magdalena, and Little Tim. Beatrice placed a granite headstone at his gravesite, honoring the man who drew the breath of the land unto himself and imagined a new life for hundreds of Afro-Americans convicts. Scores of the town's early citizens were buried on the hill, and the place became known as Old Magnolia Cemetery. It remained undisturbed for seven decades. Then in the 1980's the city sold the property to real-estate developers. All the cemetery plots and coffins were relocated, except for McGeary's, which until this day stands isolated on the edge of an affluent neighborhood. Often overgrown with vines and weeds, his headstone is a grim reminder of the early days in the land of cane.

PART TWO: SHORT STORIES

CLANCY

This story was originally written as a chapter for "In The Land Of Cane." The author found the section a hindrance to the flow of a short novel, and it now appears here, adapted and revised as a short story.

The lanky, silver-bearded one, Jake Clancy, stepped out of a crowd on the busy sidewalk and pushed through the tall double-doors of the grand Saint Anthony, a hotel recently opened in San Francisco in the year 1908. All the newspapers in California touted it as among the world's most elegant, and Clancy, having just stepped off a train from Sacramento, checked in to see for himself.

He wasn't much impressed. The hotel had a French-motif interior, and a myriad of wall mirrors in the lobby, but the place didn't compare to the grand hotels of New York or Chicago. After a day of conducting business, Clancy decided to have dinner in the hotel restaurant. Opting out of a complementary bottle of champagne, he requested a quart of his favorite brandy. Not bothering to be graceful inside the plush eatery, he unabashedly devoured a bloody steak while guzzling straight liquor. He did, however, neatly tuck the corner of a napkin inside his shirt collar, which made him appear somewhat well-mannered. When at last he burped his meal finished, the waiter arrived immediately with the check. Clancy signed for the amount due, and then he pealed off a twenty from his cash roll, handing it over to the waiter.

"Where's the game?" Clancy asked.

"Pardon me, sir," the waiter replied.

"The game," Clancy repeated. "Poker."

"Forgive me, sir," the waited begged. "But this hotel is among the world's—"

Clancy rudely interrupted. "I've slept in better hotels than this."

The comment made the waiter edgy, and it caused him to tumble a glass of crystal across Clancy's table.

The hotel manager noticed, and he crossed over to make a rescue. "I apologize for this, sir," the manager said, his hands folded piously at his breast. His tone of voice was lofty, and yet it was also serious. "May we be of further assistance?"

"Yeah," replied Clancy. "Tell me where this fine hotel's holding a poker game."

The manager grinned charmingly, but it was a false indication of his true feelings. He dismissed the waiter by a slight of hand, and then directed his attention to Clancy. "Sir, kindly follow me....."

Clancy stood and trailed the manager to his office.

"One must be discrete," the manager began. "Our hotel prides itself in both its security and confidentiality. At this moment, two hotel detectives are at work protecting the persons and interests of our guests."

"What the hell does that have to do with poker?" Clancy asked flamed with discourtesy.

The dainty manager remained unruffled. "It's a matter of collateral," he replied. "Such activities require a considerable cash guarantee."

"Money, right," Clancy deduced. "Now you're talking my language." Clancy withdrew his roll of twenties, and he lobbed it onto the manager's desk. "I figure that's three thousand. If it ain't 'considerable enough , then take a look at this." Clancy pulled his shirt up to reveal a hairy belly strapped with a cash belt. He unbuckled the belt and handed it to the awe-struck manager.

The Manager peeked curiously inside a compartment of the leather citadel, and he saw it was stuffed with hundred-dollar bills. "Very well," the manager acquiesced. "I'll locate the room."

"You do that," said Clancy. "And make sure it's high stakes."

The game was stationed on the top-floor of the hotel. No ordinary hotel room, it was actually a suite, for its manifold space was adorned with French doors and scintillating chandeliers. The terrace of the suite looked out toward the waters of the bay where polite waves rolled sleepily in the moonlight.

Clancy took a seat at a table where four players were convened. Each superlatively conducted, they greeted Clancy one-by-one. In polite fashion, they suggested that Clancy feel at home. Clancy was amused with the irony of their suggestion, for his home was an austere house outside Sacramento—a world away from ornate San Francisco, and from a penthouse suite, a full universe.

Clancy played a few inconsequential hands, forever mindful of the game's participants, studying their strengths and weaknesses. At the fourth deal of the cards, Clancy was ready to play serious poker. He opened with a pair of aces, and pushed two-thousand dollars forward. Instantly, Clancy became aware of the player's inquiring faces.

"Is there a problem, fellas?" Clancy asked.

Stunned by the boldness of Clancy's bet, the players replied in sequence:

"No."

"No."

"Of course not."

"All's fine."

Two of them dropped out of the hand, but a pair of risk-takers called and stayed in. The first player, sitting to the right of Clancy, drew only one card. His name was Sullivan, a man Clancy had heard about. A business fellow who pushed his weight around, he was rumored to be the richest man in San Francisco. Clancy easily recognized him, for he was known to wear a pair of white roses in the lapels of his tuxedos.

The gentleman to the left of Clancy requested one card just as Stanton did. His name was Wynston Sterling, but his friends called him *Wynn*. An Ivy Leaguer, he was handsome and affluent. He wore his hair slicked back and his moustache finely trimmed. On his index finger he sported a sapphire as big as a dime, and on his pinky he displayed a fine-cut diamond. Wynn smoked a cigarette with the assistance of a silver-tipped holder, sometimes smoothly puffing on it while at other times tapping it on a marble ashtray. Clancy assessed Wynn as a playboy and an amateur, recognizing that his sole method of winning was in sometimes getting lucky.

Clancy's turn to draw came now, and he told the dealer, "I'll take three." Upon receiving the cards, he gave them a cursory examination, and then he set them face-down on the table.

"Betting is open, gentlemen," the dealer announced.

Sullivan didn't hesitate to raise the stakes, and he shoved an additional one-thousand dollars into the pot. He observed Clancy in the periphery of his vision, trying to appraise his reaction. But the grey-bearded one was cagey, and he exhibited nothing to evaluate.

Clancy called and pushed a grand into the pot.

All eyes settled on the playboy. "The game's getting exuberant," Wynn declared. "I won't be left out of the fun. Therefore, I'll call." He counted out his bills atop the table and he saw they totaled only a grand. "And I'll raise *five* thousand," he added, pleased with himself. Wynn signaled to his personal assistant who reached inside his jacket, and removed an envelop thick with cash. "I believe there's ten-thousand dollars here," the playboy announced, receiving the envelope from his assistant. "I'll extract five thousand for the pot, and I'll return the other five to the vault." He delivered the envelope back over his shoulder and into his assistant's care. "Show the gentlemen my vault," Wynn instructed. The assistant unbuttoned his jacket, and opening it wide, he exposed the players' eyes to a pair of pistols: a short-barrel 38-caliber and a steely 45.

Sullivan was not entertained by the playboy's antics, and he gravely called the five thousand.

Clancy, however, announced his intention to bet further. "I'll call that five thousand and raise two thousand more." He didn't immediately tender his money, though, but sat waiting for a reaction from the other players.

"You appear to be light a few thousand dollars." Stanton uttered.

"It's not a problem," said Clancy. "Get the hotel manager up here. "He'll tell you I've got plenty cash in *my* vault."

"I'm certain you do," said Stanton, watching Clancy sign a marker for the money he owed the pot. "You couldn't have gotten in the door otherwise."

"If we all agree to call," Wynn suggested. "Then we'll have a show of cards. I find this game quite interesting."

Sullivan showed his hand. "Full house," he proclaimed. "Sevens over threes."

"You take the fun out of poker," Wynn said disheartened. "I've a king-high flush. But evidently it's not enough to beat a full house.

Sullivan readied himself to pull in his winnings, but he was thwarted by the dealer's words. "You must wait, Mr. Stanton."

The dealer was a professional, and he adroitly moved the poker game forward. "Mr. Clancy will proceed."

Sullivan was incredulous, for the odds were in his favor, and they indicated Clancy would lose the hand. "He's nothing to beat a full house," the political boss asserted. "The man drew three cards. It's tough for anyone to be that lucky." Once again, Sullivan eagerly reached for the pot.

"I must insist, Mr. Sullivan," the dealer instructed.

Sullivan sat back and colonized his chair.

Clancy flipped his cards into the center of the table. They laid face up, but they weren't completely discernable.

The dealer spread out Clancy's cards by a stroke of his index finger. "Full house," he announced. "Aces over nines."

Sullivan struggled to maintain his composure. Exasperated, he had to calmly watch Clancy reel in twenty-thousand-dollars in winnings

Ernest Phillips, a bespectacled mid-west banker who had stayed silent throughout the game, wiped the sweat on to his neck. "That was quite exciting," he said.

"Oh, yes," the playboy chimed. "Loosing money can be very exciting—when it's someone else's cash." The table muttered with cultured laughter, except for Sullivan, who sullenly sipped a drink, hoping to recoup his losses with the following hand.

Once again the dealer began to deal.

"So, where are you from, Mr. Clancy?" the banker asked in a friendly, off-handed way.

"Just about everywhere, I imagine," Clancy replied.

"That's rather cryptic," the playboy commented. "Don't you agree?"

"You folks sure use some fancy words," said Clancy.

"It's a product of our upbringing," the banker explained.

"We can't do anything about it," Wynn confessed.

"It don't bother me none," Clancy assured the men.

"We appreciate that," said Sullivan acerbically.

The dealer cared little for conversation. "It's your bet, Mr. Clancy," he said, directing the players' attention back to the game.

"I'll check," Clancy responded.

"He checks?"

"Yes, he does."

"Perhaps we'll have a chance this hand."

"I'm certainly ready," said Wynn, hoping for a better outcome than last time.

The banker pushed one-thousand dollars into the pot and all the other players followed. "Clancy, Clancy," the banker enunciated. "The name's familiar. Any chance you're from Los Angeles?"

"No, I'm a country boy," Clancy replied.

"I once heard about a fellow in Los Angeles," the banker continued. "He owned a god-awful amount of land. He cultivated everything—cotton, corn, oranges. He had more than a thousand Mexicans working for him. Of course, he paid them next to nothing, and he made himself a fortune. Then one day he just walked away from it all. Sold his land cheap to the Mexicans and just disappeared."

"Only a fool would do such a thing," Sullivan commented. "I'd like to get that man in a game of cards."

The players at the table laughed, except Clancy, who sat silent and serene, like a cold midnight snow.

The banker tried to escalate Clancy's temperature. "I'm in for another thousand." he announced.

Each player followed the banker's lead, but not Clancy. He merely inspected his cards, peering at them with a countenance of indecision. "Excuse me, gentlemen," he finally said. "I forgot to telegraph my wife." He set down his cards and stood up. "We'll meet another time. You'll have a fair chance to win your money back."

Stanton studied Clancy. "What's the problem?" he asked. "You don't expect to win big on every hand, do you?"

"It's not the cards," Clancy replied.

"Then stay and play," Sullivan suggested. "Write a message to your wife. Wynn's man will take it down to the telegraph office. He'll see that all is handled properly." Sullivan leaned forward, placing his hands firmly on the poker table. "I'm asking nicely," he added. "Even though I'm not an altogether nice person."

Clancy recognized the threat. Pulling up his shirt, he unloosened his cash belt and dropped it into the center of the table. "I'm in," he declared.

"How much is there, Mr. Clancy?" the dealer asked.

"To the dollar?" Clancy asked in turn.

"Just the neighborhood," Sullivan answered glibly.

"Twenty thousand," Clancy informed the players.

"I'm sorry," the dealer apologized. "The limit is five-thousand dollars."

"Fine," Clancy responded. "I'll bet my twenty against anyone's five."

The playboy laughed. "Sounds like a real bargain," he said merrily.

"You haven't yet drawn a card," Sullivan reminded Clancy.

"I'll stay with the ones I have," the grey-bearded one stated.

"He's bluffing," Sullivan warned.

"Perhaps," spoke the banker. "But the stakes are too rich for me."

The playboy shrugged affably. "Oh, what the hell. It's only money," he said.

Sullivan boldly pushed in five thousand. "I'm in," he said, not so much with arrogance as confidence. "And I'll draw one card."

The dealer dealt Sullivan a single card. "There's no reason for further betting," he said. "Mr. Clancy accepted Mr. Sullivan's five-thousand-dollars against his bet of twenty thousand."

Clancy passed his cards to the dealer who opened them for inspection. "Mr. Clancy has four sevens," the dealer announced for the benefit of everyone present.

Sullivan slammed his cards upon the table. "Damn it!" he cried out. "Clancy, we'd think you were a cheat, but this is our dealer!" The reality of the situation now rendered Sullivan speechless. Crumbling back into his chair, he cursed wildly. "I'll be damned! Damned!"

"Guess I'll be heading out," Clancy told the players. "Unless anyone objects."

The players said not a word, but simply watched as Clancy stuffed his pockets with cash. Clancy stepped away to leave, but the dealer delayed his exit.

"Do you want an escort from hotel security?" he asked.

"It won't be necessary," replied Clancy. He then walked away mundanely, as if the events of the passed hour happened to him everyday.

Wynn's assistant leaned down and whispered to his boss, something to the effect that the cash he lost could be expeditiously recovered.

"Leave him be," Wynn instructed the man. "He beat us fairly, and he entertained us as well. Besides, I think he's that fellow from Los Angeles....."

Wynn grinned The other players resigned themselves to their losses, and they broke into smiles. Sullivan, however, sat brooding.

"Oh, come now, Stanton," said Wynn, a tenor of joy in his voice. "It could have been much worse."

"How's that?" asked Stanton.

"He could have beaten us on a bluff."

Wynn laughed, and the players joined in, even Sullivan, who reached for a bottle of whiskey, and finding its seal unbroken, he twisted it free by a clamp of his teeth.

TEACHERS

This nonfiction story is a recollection of four teachers of M.D. Shannon from middle school thru graduate studies.

The first teacher to profoundly impress me was a rather tragic figure. When I was ten-years of age, my life was transplanted from Texas to North Philadelphia, and here I attended Bayard Taylor School (note 5), a three-floor school house built of iron, brick and rough-hewn stone.

I'll call the teacher Mr. Hall, but that's not his name, for though he's certainly deceased by now, I don't wish to disparage him in any way. Bayard Taylor was a typical city school of the day, combining the academics of math and science with a vocational program. Mr. Hall taught woodshop and mechanical drawing. For the most part, my classmates and I diligently applied ourselves in Mr. Hall's classes, but that doesn't mean we weren't prone to cutting up now and then. Mr. Hall was usually friendly, but his tolerances had their limits. One day, having too long endured our antics in woodshop, he called me before the class, and he asked me what seemed to be an absurdly comical question. "Do you want to see Santa Claus?" he inquired. The moment he uttered those words I knew that I was in serous trouble, but there was nothing I could do to avoid the inevitable. The glare in his eyes informed me that I would soon see *Santa Claus*. Using his thumbs and index fingers, Mr. Hall took hold of the hairs around the area of my temples, and holding them tightly, he lifted me up onto the balls of my feet. Though I was standing on the tips of my toes, he continued to lift me, ever so slightly, creating a wrenching, eye-watering pain in my scalp. While I hadn't reached the point of sobbing, I did yelp like a dog, and fortunately for me, that was enough for him to gently let me down. As I shamefully trudged back to my place in class, my classmates watched me, their faces agape, and their eyes sympathetic. Needless to say, it was a long time before there was any misconduct in Mr. Hall's woodshop.

I attended Mr. Hall's mechanical drawing class for three years on a twice-weekly basis. The class work was quite satisfying, and I found it a peasant departure from my regular classes that had periodic tests and assigned homework. Mr. Hall's class activities were quite different. He simply introduced a new concept or object, and the class tried their hands at mastering it. In my third year of mechanical drawing, my classmates and I found ourselves doing very advanced work. Although my progress with complex drawings was merely average, I had a level of comfort with the class, which I didn't have with my others.

At the time, I had a part-time job at a small fruit-and-vegetable store across the street from my house. I worked an hour each morning before school and a couple hours in the afternoon. I had mechanical drawing for my first class-period, which meant that I went directly from my job to Mr. Hall's classroom. It was not uncommon for me to eat a pear or apple for breakfast, sometimes nibbling the fruit while in the store, and at other times while walking to school. On one particular occasion, I put an apple in my jacket pocket, and headed off to Bayard Taylor. Absorbed in ruminations about trivial things, I forgot about the apple until I reached the steps of the school. I began to consume it, despite the fact that I was not too far from the door of Mr. Hall's classroom.

I entered the class while biting into the apple, and I strolled toward my drawing desk. What followed was unexpected. I was suddenly halted by Mr. Hall's voice. "What are you doing?" he asked. The question caught me off guard, and as I hadn't any idea what he referred to, I replied with something that sounded insubordinate, which was not uncommon for me, but I don't believe it was my intention in this case. Mr. Hall reacted by angrily crossing over to me. He slapped away the apple with one hand, and with his other hand he slapped the side of my face. It wasn't a terribly strong slap, but I was standing near the blackboard and my head knocked against it, momentarily dizzying me. I recovered and glanced curiously at Mr. Hall. How strange, I thought, for his face wore an incongruent expression of regret and satisfaction.

I took my place at my desk amid icy silence. Nothing was ever mentioned regarding the incident, except by my friends who wanted to know if the slap had hurt. Yeah, sure, but the violent act hurt my pride more than anything else.

A few years later, I went back to Bayard Taylor and visited my former teachers. I made it a point to see Mr. Hall, and I found him at work in his woodshop. He was alone, and I went in. We exchanged greetings and exchanged small talk. However, I saw that Mr. Hall's demeanor was different, for his hands trembled, and his eyes were unsteady. I felt sorry for the man, for something had adversely affected him. I didn't know what it was, and I didn't dare ask. Looking back on those days, though, I must consider that his life was probably similar with my own life. I was challenged and confused by the world around me. Crime, drug-addiction, and violence were rampant in the inner-city, and their reality profoundly influenced me. I didn't have any idea about Mr. Hall's personal life back then, but I do know he lived in a far nicer neighborhood than I did. However, that simple fact didn't save him from experiencing the vagaries of life. In the grand scope of things, he was no different from me. We were both humans, and therefore, we had human frailties. Try as he might have to mask his frailties, he was unable to prohibit others from perceiving his soul, to keep them from seeing the anguished child that lay within him.

With all due respect to Mr. Hall as a teacher, a few of my classmates excelled in mechanical drawing and were sufficiently prepared to go on to successful careers. At least one of my classmates entered the city's best technical high school, and he was immediately accelerated two grades. He earned a scholarship to Drexel University, and while he was always a bright kid, I seriously doubt he could have gone so far so quickly if not for Mr. Hall's adroit tutelage.

Many teachers throughout the years impress us, but a precious few make impressions that influence our future and affect the very nature of our existence. One such teacher of mine was in the tenth grade, an English teacher of apparently common talents, but actually one of extraordinary gifts. I will forever hold her in high regard for what she shared with me, and how she influenced my intellectual life and creative world. I don't remember her name, for I had only the briefest interactions with her. As far as she was concerned, I was merely one more face in a crowd of pupils, another name in a grade book. I don't begrudge her for that, for she was a teacher who dealt with her classes realistically and with pragmatic methods. If her students were predisposed for literary discussions, then she provided the conditions to make it happen. Likewise, if she perceived that her students were void of any interest in the regular study of literature, she provided the conditions for which her students could learn in a vastly different manner.

My class pertained to the latter. It didn't take our teacher long to see the necessity for setting aside established English activities and replacing them with one small book. I don't infer that she distributed copies of one lone book for us to read, for there was only *one* copy of this book, and *she* was the only person who did any reading. We simply sat and listened as she read, this young teacher, a seemingly ordinary woman who wore black-rim glasses—but a woman of sublime emphasis, having a voice to compare with the voices of muses.

As the days passed, I and my classmates became increasingly enthralled with her voice and the book's unfolding story. We sat silently, hardly moving, some girls polishing their nails while boys sometimes twisted their necks to check out the hemline of a girl's skirt. However, we were all quiet, as if we were part of some churchlike holiness, and any needless sound would disrupt the sanctity of the room to become an unpardonable sin.

The book was William Saroyan's *The Human Comedy*, a simple, thoughtful story of a young boy named Homer who worked part-time at the local telegraph office during World War II. Sometimes Homer had to deliver messages to the parents of recently-fallen sons, and each message was heart-wrenching. The story is endearing and poetic, both in its words and its meaning. It is said that Saroyan wrote the book to give hope during the war. As my class was a part of a generation born after the war, we therefore had no first-hand knowledge of it. However, the connection that the book made between us and a world we had not previously known was immeasurable. For me, that measure has spanned a half-century, and is unending even to this day. The metaphors, references and allusion of Saroyan's book are imbued with the genius of the classical work *The Odyssey*. The names of Saroyan's characters, the town, and theme of *The Human Comedy* brings into modern story the timelessness of life's joy and suffering. Little did I know that two decades later I would write a libretto based on a section in ancient Homer's epic story *The Odyssey*. How very strange life is, for timeless things abide with us, leading us toward an unknown future.

I would never learn what my classmates took away for themselves from our classroom experience, for I dropped out of school before the Christmas holidays, and never again returned to high school. I instead entered a cold, harsh world—a darkness embedded with the angst of living and dying, the eternal, inescapable comedy of the human condition.

Many years later, when I entered college, quite a few teachers imparted valuable ideas and knowledge to me, but it wasn't until I attended The University of Texas at Austin that I discovered teachers who impacted my life in expanded ways. Doctor Paul Gray, a distinguished Professor of the Performance of Literature, was gracious with his time, and he often counseled me about performing poetry. It was obvious that I had only minute experience compared with other students, many of whom had seriously studied literature and drama since high school. Professor Gray often spoke to me about a "break through"— when a performer or actor breaks from "acting" and actually becomes the character, or in the case of performing poetry, the actor becomes the voice of the poem. Both he and I were concerned with my lack of progress in performing. Then something happened.

Class members usually selected the poems they would perform from a list, and once a student selected a particular poem, it became unavailable to other students. On one occasion, I delayed too long in selecting a poem, and not many remained to select from. I felt the poems that were available were either too long in length, or had inaccessible content, both of which would prove difficult for me to perform. I had no recourse but to select T.S. Eliot's *Ash Wednesday*, an enigmatic poem about Eliot's religious conversion. The Poem is rife with biblical allusions, and its voice is one of agony and disillusionment.

I spent a great deal of time reading *Ash Wednesday* and in practicing for a performance of it. By degrees, I began to hear the poem's essential voice, and while many of the poem's allusions were unclear to be, I intensely felt its rhythms and images. When it came time to perform the poem in class, I felt comfortable, and I believed I could successfully get through it.

Class days that were set aside for student performances were always met with both excitement and anxiety. The overall objective of the class, of course, was the refinement of students' performance skills, and yet many of my classmates had already reached a high level of proficiency. When my turn came, I stepped up to the podium, and I felt the presence of my peers weighing down on me. *Ash Wednesday* begins with a few seemingly rambling phrases, and though I had not anticipated this, the lines fell nervously from my lips, and it soon became apparent to everyone that this might be the most pathetic performance of a poem they ever witnessed. Thoughts flashed through my mind, informing me of my doubts and fears. I felt utterly inept and hopelessly unprepared to perform the poem, and moreover, the result would probably mean my having to find another field of study. Suddenly something came over me, and the tenor of my voice changed. It was as if my fear, which had redoubled with each word I spoke, was affected by the poem's emotions. My voice became the poet's voice, and somehow, most inextricably, I was expressing the poet's emotions. I wasn't in control of the performance, however, for I was simply a conduit for a force that was not mine. I didn't dare lift my eyes from the text—not for a moment; for I feared I would lose my connection with the poem. Despite my not looking at the audience, I knew they were enraptured, for it was impossible to attend that classroom and not be overwhelmed by the power of the poet's voice.

My performance of *Ash Wednesday* ended, and I returned to my seat. It was customary in Professor Gray's class that no comments were given. However, after class Professor Gray approached me in the hallway, and sharing a scholarly, good-natured laugh, he said, "yeah, that was certainly a breakthrough." He was right, for in the future I became increasingly comfortable with the performance of literature.

All was not idyllic, though, for the next semester I had great trouble with a required course that dealt exclusively with scholarly analysis—with criticism, metrical forms, and so forth. I was not a student of high intellect, and if the truth be known, my grades were sometimes less than average. I was handicapped, of course, for I hadn't attended high school, and instead I had gotten a General Equivalency Diploma. I then attended a community college in order to obtain a non qualifying entrance into The University. I abysmally failed my first exam in Professor Gray's analysis class, and I feared I would fail the course itself. My only hope was in doing an optional special project for additional credit, and I immersed myself in completing one.

I had written a few poems at the time, and some of them had good qualities, so I figured I would write a poem for Professor Gray, and perhaps, he would look kindly upon it. The poem (note 6) referenced my plight and inability to comprehend scholarly analysis. Once the poem was written, I was satisfied, for it was an amusing, heart-felt piece. However, I didn't know how Professor Gray would receive it. I visited him during his office hours, and I told him I had completed a special project. Placing the poem in his hands, I watched as he began to read it. He abruptly stopped, though, and handing the poem back to me, he said, "perform it for me." I did, and he was delighted with the poem. I was flattered when he told me he would keep it among his personal papers. He smiled and thanked me, and I went off merrily, knowing my class grade would increase considerably. Professor Gray, though, abided with much academic integrity, and his generosity had its limits. My final grade was a "C", and frankly, that was more than I deserved.

Rarely are students so fortunate as to attend classes by a pre-imminent figure in their field of study, and I was exceedingly privileged to enroll in two graduate-level courses taught by Richard Howard (note 7), the renowned poet, critic, editor and translator.

A Pulitzer-Prize winner and a MacArthur Award recipient, Howard's lectures were brilliant; and in the late 1970's at The University of Texas, he was quite an enthralling character. We were a small class of perhaps twenty students along with a few professors, all gathered to attend the great man's talks, which were woven with poignant insights and personal anecdotes. The central theme of his lectures was "the female will." Howard sourced his idea back to the British poet Christopher Smart, a somewhat tragic poet of the mid-seventeenth century, and he traced the concept forward through various poets and literary eras, finalizing his lectures with a discussion of Oscar Wilde whose life, like Smart's, ended shortly after a dreadful term in prison.

It's impossible to define Howard's idea of the *female will* in a few short phrases, but perhaps it will suffice to say it references a feminine gift-giving muse—one of unknowable volitions. Howard must have seen his own work as influenced by the *female will*. I vividly recall him at the head of the class, casually leaning against the front of his desk, puffing on a thin, extra-long cigarette, his hand daintily extended as he explicated a novel view or concept. His voice was mellow and sublime, and it was quite pleasant to listen to. He performed only one of his poems in class, as I recall, but that one performance was enormously special. The poem was titled *Lot Later*, a monologue about the well-known biblical figure who fled the destruction of Sodom and Gomorrah.

The following semester I attended my second course with Richard Howard. It was a performance-based class that included members of Austin's theater community. The class publicly performed Oscar Wilde's *Salome*, a play which Howard had translated, and as he conveyed to us, Wilde wrote in French *for* the French. The nuance was something that Howard sometimes gave to words to express an idea that he could not otherwise express without a deep discourse.

I didn't have an acting role in the play *Salome*, for I was appointed assistant director. Richard Howard was selected for the role of Herod, despite his confession that he had no dramatic experience. However, he was ideal for the role, and he played his part quite well.

The production of the play was superb in color and staging. Herod sat on his opulent throne commanding edicts, surrounded by exquisite slaves and attendants, some with vans of palms fanning their royal Majesty. The story of Salome is well-known, and there is a section in the play where Herod becomes yoked by the reality of his having beheaded John the Baptist. It is a crucial scene, and Howard played it adequately. However, something transpired one evening to transform this adequacy into a superlative dramatic performance.

It was quite warm in the old Sixth Street theater, which was fine with the director, for the natural setting of the play was tepid. Many of the characters were directed to dab the sweat on their faces using props of silky kerchiefs. Pivotal in the scene was the moment when Herod stepped wearily away from his throne and took center stage where he delivered an anguished soliloquy. During the scene, Howard's performance suddenly became affected by the awful temperature of the stage, and he appeared to be overcome by it. Sweat poured down his face, and he became visibly drained. His dramatic pauses were longer than normal, his breath was labored, and his limbs were heavy. Exhausted, he crossed back to his throne, and he fell into it dizzily. All was immaculately still, except for the motions of the vans, which refreshed the air, allowing Howard to continue his speech, which had now become profuse, emotive and profound.

Of course, I mentioned nothing of the event to Howard. For though his presence among us was informal, and he was accessible, the status we appointed to him was exalted. He had not asked for this status, but I'm certain he preferred it this way, for personally, I felt he agonized over small talk, and he would much rather have literary dialogue with a scholarly equal than to speak mundanely with a mere mortal.

Such must be the encumbrance of an intellectual genius.

Speaking for myself, I have only an average intellect, but I consider it a great fortune to have witnessed the gifts of Richard Howard. I don't know what place Howard will have in literary history, but I do know the place he maintains in my memory, and the influence he has had on my own writings.

LA ESPERANZA

La Esperanza is a short story from a collection of interrelated stories titled "Tales from The Snakeskin Journal" (note 7).

The aircraft landed outside the city of La Esperanza beneath a clouded sky, and it taxied to a terminal where its passengers exited onto a concourse. One man, though, dressed in a business suit, stepped down onto the tarmac alone, pacing soldierly toward a waiting black sedan. He was met at the door of the car by Professor Alfonso De Deon, an internationally-recognized figure in the field of economics and a recently selected winner of the Nobel Prize. The two men entered the car, and they sat together on the rear seat, separated by a leather fold-down arm rest. "I wasn't told your name," Del Leon said. "Only that you were coming to help. However, without knowing anything about you, I must wonder about your motive."

The professor peered out over the rims of his eyeglasses. "Your government has never wanted to help until now," he added. "There wasn't any need to help," responded the man.

"That doesn't answer anything," the professor said, his gazed firmly fixed. "I want to know your name, and I want to know your position in the government." "My name is Marcos Gallegos," the man replied. "And

181

I have a position in the intelligence community."

"I'm surprised you're so candid," Del Leon said. "Government agents are not always welcome in La Esperanza."

Marcos sat in silence for a moment. "I can understand why you find it difficult to trust me," he finally said. "I'm an intelligence agent, but I have an allegiance to an organization with ideals that oppose my government's. At this point, there's little I can say to remove any doubts you have. Perhaps tomorrow you'll see things differently."

"What will happen tomorrow?" asked Del Leon.

"The Vice President will arrive."

"But he's not expected to arrive until the day after tomorrow."

"He'll arrive before dawn tomorrow, and he'll convene a meeting between the intelligence community and his senior staff. I'll attend the meeting."

The black sedan rolled out of the airport, and it glided onto the highway where it sped toward a turnoff that led into the mountains.

"I've made reservations at a hotel in the city," Marcos informed the professor..

"You'll say at my estate in the country," Del Leon responded. "You'll be comfortable there."

"And you'll be able to keep an eye on me," Marcos guessed.

"That's correct," Del Leon agreed. "I'll keep an eye on you."

The professor's country estate was surrounded by miles of vineyards, and beyond the main house stretched a row of winery facilities. The entrance to the estate was guarded by peasants armed with rifles. The main house and its cottages were watched over by a group of casually-dressed young men whom Marcos guessed were students.

Marcos looked out over the spacious vineyards. "It's more than an ordinary country estate," he said.

"Ten-thousand acres," the professor explained. "It was my father's, and his father's before him. After you've rested from your journey, I'll show you around. Then we'll have dinner, and a bottle of wine, of course."

Later that afternoon, Marcos rode with the professor in a horse-drawn wagon though acres of vineyards, the professor telling his guest about the growing of vines. After a brief visit to a wine-processing facility, the two men returned to the main house and had a dinner of peasant soup and skewered goat. They consumed their meal in veritable silence, but after dinner they sat out on the veranda, and while smoking cigars, they spoke unguardedly.

"This in my home," Professor Del Leon said. "And it is the place where my theories on cultural economics began. My experience here taught me that an economic system must be interrelated with the culture of its people. It doesn't matter how large or small a society is, for its economy is necessarily a function of culture. To deny this means to deny a society its essence, its history and identity."

"I'm not a man of intellect," Marcos replied. "I don't quite understand cultural economics. I leave the development of theories to others. I deal with practical matters, with strategy and operations."

They sat in the stillness of the evening, and after they had finished their cigars, Professor Del Leon suggested that they retire. Marcos left the house and headed toward his cottage, which was some distance away. Strolling along a gravel pathway, he passed a pond where a young woman lingered beneath a mossy tree.

"You must be the man everyone is talking about," she said.

Marcos stopped strolling and addressed her. "Perhaps," he answered. "But I don't know what people are. saying."

The woman let out a blithe, endearing laugh. "My name is Lorena," she said, introducing herself. "I'm a graduate student at the university. My cottage is over there." She pointed, and Marcos saw that her cottage was adjacent to his. "It's beautiful in the country, don't you agree?" she asked. Marcos watched as Lorena stepped out of the shadow of the tree and into the moonlight. A slender woman, she had long, black shimmering hair, a graceful body, and a face adorned with a warm smile. "What's your name," she asked. Marcos told her his name, but he said nothing more. "It's sometimes lonely here," Lorena added. "It's nice to have a visitor."

Marcos recognized her as a temptress, and yet he felt she was an innocuous one. "Would you like to have a brandy before turning in for the night?" he asked her.

"I'd love to, Lorena replied.

Taking hold of Marco's arm, Lorena walked beside him toward his cottage. Stepping inside, Lorena got comfortable on the sofa, folding her legs lady-like on a cushion. Marcos removed a bottle of brandy from the bar, and poured Lorena a drink. After pouring himself a brandy, he sat in a chair across from her and waited for the inevitable questions.

"You're not Hispanic, are you?" she asked.

"Why do you ask?" Marcos responded.

"You don't appear to be," she replied. "Is Marcos Gallegos your birth name?"

"It's my name," he answered. "It's all that matters."

"But it wasn't always your name, was it?" she asked.

"If my name was John Doe," Marcos said. "Would it make any difference?"

"Perhaps," Lorena replied.

Marcos reached inside his jacket and withdrew a government credential. He tossed it to Lorena, and it landed on her lap. "Take a look," he suggested. "I'm precisely who I say I am. I'll tell you nothing more about myself. I'll certainly not tell you anything about my past, for I won't comprise the safety of anyone who knows me. I'm sure your training taught you that."

Lorena was effectively disarmed. "Well, I don't quite know what to say," she uttered, unnerved by Marcos frank comments. She lifted her glass, which was now empty, and gestured for Marcos to refill it.

Marcos was in no mood for games. He stood and reached for her glass, but instead of taking the glass from her hand, he grasped her wrist and pulled her resolutely off the sofa, spinning her toward the cottage door. "Tell Professor Del Leon that I find it a professional discourtesy that he sends a woman to ask me questions. He should ask the questions himself. Now, if you don't mind, I have an early meeting in the city, and I'd like to get some sleep."

The meeting convened before dawn the next morning. The Vice President met with his senior staff and select members of the intelligence community in an elegant conference room in a downtown hotel.

"Most us know the reason for this meeting," the Vice President began. "Our Global Enterprise has found considerable opposition with Doctor Del Leon and his popular theory of cultural economics. Frankly, I don't know what in hell's name his theory is all about, except that everyone says it doesn't support globalization. In two days, the League of Twenty Nations will vote on the most important global initiative of our generation. A vote of confidence there will make way for the creation of a world-wide economic system, which will become the foundation for a global government. We meet here this morning to develop a strategy to neutralize the opposition. It's imperative that we do this, for if we don't, the League of Twenty Nations may vote against globalization and set the initiative back a full decade." The Vice President paused and sipped a glass of water. "I'm asking for ideas," he added.

"Why not shoot the bastard?" a voice proffered.

The attendees laughed, and the atmosphere became more relaxed.

"We all know that a dead martyr is more powerful than a living person," the Vice President said grimly.

A pale of silence descended. Then a hand rose up from the crowd, the hand of a woman. She was dressed in a ladies business suit, and she wore a naval ring on her finger. "Mr. Vice President," she said respectfully. "I've spent the last few weeks reading Del Leon's work, and I must tell you, his cultural economic theories are rather ambiguous."

"That's no surprise," the Vice President commented.

"Yes sir," the woman agreed. "And I believe it's possible to capitalize on that."

"Continue," the Vice President said, encouraging the woman to speak.

"I believe the appropriate strategy is to agree with Del Leon's theories rather than argue against them. The only people who really understand Del Leon's work are intellectuals; the masses merely understand his concepts as a few ideals and benefits." The woman glanced around the room at her peers, and then she turned her eyes back toward the Vice President. "Tomorrow you'll deliver a speech at the International Economic Conference.

Embrace Del Leon's economic theories. Inform the world that the Global Enterprise is indebted to Del Leon's work, and that cultural economics is important within the scope of globalization. It doesn't matter that they aren't. It only matters that people believe they are. Sooner or later the masses will discover that Del Leon's work is actually in opposition to globalization. But that will be too late."

The Vice President approved, and he nodded his head for the go-ahead.

Marcos departed the meeting and strolled out of the lobby alone. The black sedan waited for him at the curb of the hotel's entrance, and Marcos slipped in the rear door. The sedan pulled away and navigated through heavy traffic, arriving to a busy intersection where its door opened, and Professor Del Leon got in. .

"I apologize for last evening," the professor began. "It was poor judgment on my part. I realize now that I must trust you— for better or worse. The future of the world may rest in your hands."

"No, Professor," Marcos replied. "I'm afraid the fate of the world cannot be changed."

"What do you mean?" Del Leon asked curiously.

Marcos peered gravely at the professor. "I've just learned that the Vice President will embrace your Theory of Cultural Economics."

The professor was bewildered. "He can't possibly do that. Cultural Economics is the antithesis of globalization."

"He can do it, and he will," Marcos explained. "Tomorrow in his speech at the conference. There's nothing I can do to stop him. His speech will gain the support he needs."

That night, Marcos lay awake in his cottage. He could not sleep, for he was thinking how he could help the opposition. After hours of agonizing, he suddenly sat up in bed. An idea came to him, an idea that would certainly work. However, he was unsure if Professor Del Leon would ensure its success.

Marcos got out of bed, and slipping into a robe, he went outside and knocked on the door of Lorena's cottage. She answered sleepy-eyed, her hands holding the neck of her nightgown close to her body.

"Go to the main house and awaken Professor Del Leon," Marcos ordered her. "Tell him to come to my cottage. I must speak with him immediately."

Within a period of twenty minutes, Lorena and the professor arrived at Marcos' cottage. Marcos showed them inside, and everyone sat in the living room where logs burned in a fireplace.

"There's a possibility," Marcos began. "We may be able to turn the tide against the globalization initiative. But Professor, it will be quite difficult for you to do what I suggest."

"I will do anything within my power," the professor responded. "The globalization initiative must be stopped."

"Tomorrow you must deliver a speech at the economic conference," Marcos informed him.

"No, I'm not scheduled to speak for another few days," Del Leon explained.

"That'll be too late," Marcos said. "You must speak tomorrow—after the Vice President's address."

"Perhaps it can be arranged," Del Leon said. "But what can I possible say to change things?"

"Renounce your theories of cultural economics," Marcos declared. "You must repudiate your ideas before the entire world."

"He can't do that," Lorena objected. "You're asking him to renounce his life's work."

"Indeed, I am," agreed Marcos. "But there's no other way."

Professor Del Leon stood up, a shade of dread drawn down over his face. He solemnly exited the cottage and trudged along the pathway back to the main house accompanied by Lorena.

The following day, when the Vice President took the podium at the conference, Marcos was in attendance. His eyes searched the auditorium for Del Leon, but he didn't find him among the conference participants.

Television cameras suspended from the ceiling lowered down and zoomed in on the Vice President. "Thank you for inviting me to speak at this important conference," he began. "As most of you know, I am a proponent of the global initiative. Globalization is an idea that has abided with us for quite some time. No one knows for certain where it precisely began. Perhaps it started when a compassionate soul peered into the sad eyes of a hungry family, or perhaps it was the sight of hundreds of homeless children sleeping on the cold ground. Wherever it began is unimportant. It is important, though, that the time for globalization has finally come. There are many whom we must thank, in particular, Doctor Alfonso Del Leon. His Nobel Prize-winning work in Cultural Economics has inspired those who work tirelessly on the global initiative. His brilliant work has helped make globalization a reality, and his contribution will be remembered by all future generations."

Marcos hung his head. When the speech was at last finished, the conference host introduced Professor Del Leon. As he walked out from backstage, applause went up from the audience, and it soon grew into an ovation.

Once the applause softened, the professor began to speak. "Ladies and gentlemen, officials of governments, and esteemed colleagues, welcome to this important conference. However, it is with great regret I am here to speak with you." The audience murmured, puzzled by the professor's words. "I must say something that I should have said long ago. I've dedicated my life to Cultural Economics. But unfortunately, during the last few years, I discovered that my theories are misguided, for they have many errors. My ideas are hopelessly unworkable. In fact, Cultural Economics will be a detriment to society. Therefore, I ask you to discard my theories." Professor Del Leon paused a long moment before continuing. "Forgive me for having delayed so long in telling you this. But you must understand, I am an old man who has spent his life working on something that is worthless, and it's been difficult for me to accept it." The professor bravely lifted his eyes to the audience. "The time has come to say goodbye. I wish you all the best, and I hope that you find some good work—work that is not connected with Cultural Economics."

Professor Del Leon stepped away from the podium and disappeared backstage. News reporters scrambled up the aisles, anxious to report on what they heard. They knew that Del Leon's speech had damaged the cause of globalization, and it would be worldwide news. Marcos too departed the auditorium. Passing through the hotel lobby, he strolled outdoors into the streets of La Esperanza. Ignoring the black sedan that waited for him, he hailed a taxi and returned to the airport.

THE ORPHAN

This story is also taken from the collection titled "Tales From The Snakeskin Journal."

Freelance photographer Tony Obscuro was respected for his talent in obtaining gory photos of corpuses and the bloodied bodies of accident victims. After a long weekend of shooting, he hustled up the stairs of his East Los Angles apartment building and entered his abode, a roll of undeveloped film in hand. Kicking aside an ashtray on the floor, he dropped the strap of his Nikon from his shoulder and set it on the sofa. He then went into his bedroom closet, which he used as a darkroom, and began developing a roll of 35-millimeter film. Once finished, Tony hung his contact sheet up to dry and clicked off an infra-red lamp. Exhausted from the weekend, he slipped out of the closet and lay down on a mattress on the floor, quietly dozing off to sleep.

Three hours later he awakened. Freshening up by splashing water on his face, he sat down with his laptop and scribed a few short paragraphs about the photos he had just developed. After collecting his things and stuffing them into a vinyl briefcase, he slicked back his hair and donned a plaid sport coat. Going outdoors, he hopped in his orange Firebird and sped off to the office of the tabloid The National Exploiter.

"Hey, Boss," Tony announced as he came in the door. "I got the photos I told you about."

"Great," replied Tony's editor. "Let's take a look."

Tony reached into his briefcase, and drawing out his contact sheet, he placed it into his editor's hands.

"So this is him, hu?" the editor surmised. "Boyce Belder, the famous movie star." Shifting his cigar from one side of his mouth to the other, he spoke in a probing manner. "He looks different dead, but most corpses are like that."

"What do you think of my shot of him when he was alive?" Tony asked.

"Yeah, it's kind of strange," the editor replied. "I guess you had some problems in the darkroom."

"No," Tony contested. "Everything went fine."

"Then what's this fuzzy stuff?" asked the editor, closely examining the photos with a magnifying glass. "All your photos of Boyce Belder have some kind of washout or something."

"It ain't no washout," Tony responded. "I tried telling you about it over the phone. But you didn't listen."

"Oh, yeah," the editor recollected. "What was it you called it?"

"An aura," Tony replied.

"Yeah, that's right," said the editor. "You said Boyce Belder had an aura." He sucked on his cigar and then removed it from his mouth. "You know, a lot of tabloid stuff's been done about auras. It ain't interesting no more."

Tony reached into his briefcase and pulled out a sheet of paper. "Well, maybe you'll find this interesting," he said.

"What's this?" asked the editor, glancing at the paper.

"It my story for The Exploiter," Tony replied proudly. "It explains everything about Boyce Belder's aura." Tony rested his forearm on the editor's desk and leaned forward. "You see, Boss," he added. "It's all about electro-magnetic energy."

The editor gazed curiously at Tony. "Well, I guess I should read the story," he said.

"Yeah," Tony agreed. "You got to read it."

The editor lifted the story to his face and read its lead paragraph aloud. "Alien beings from some unknown existence are on the earth in human bodies doing good and evil. Boyce Belder was an alien, and the proof of this is the electro-magnetic energy surrounding his body." The editor rubbed his chin. "Wow, you got some imagination."

"I didn't imagine nothing," said Tony. "It's the truth."

"Really?" the editor quizzed.

"That's right," said Tony. "The truth."

"Look, kid," the editor began. "We've all been through our truth-in-journalism stages some sometimes in our careers. But it's just a stage. You'll get over it."

"So, you're not going to print my story?" Tony asked, aching with the thought of rejection.

The editor appeared sympathetic. "Look, Tony," he began. "I know you want to get a story into The Exploiter—you've always wanted to be a real journalist. But on this story it ain't possible. What you got is too far out. Noboby's gonna believe it."

"So what are you gonna do about astory?" Tony asked. "The Exploiter's got to have a story to go with my photos."

"The police say Boyce Belder was robbed and murdered," the editor replied. "We're gonna go with that angle."

"But it ain't true!" Tony exclaimed. "He was killed by his brother, Josh Belder!"

The editor sighed. "You got to understand," the editor said. "Everybody knows Boyce Belder had no family. He didn't have a brother."

"He had a brother!" Tony cried. "I met him. He's the guy who told me everything—about electro-magnetic energy, and how Boyce Belder is an evil alien!"

"Where's Josh now?" asked the editor. "I'd like to have a talk with him."

"I don't know where he is," Tony replied. "He vanished."

"Vanished?" asked the editor incredulously.

"Yeah," Tony shot back. "And I got an eye-witness that saw him vanish. Her name's Doreen."

"Forget it," the editor suggested. "You mentioned something about this Doreen girl on the phone. You said she was a blond, and she was a little goofy. Look, Tony, it's a dead-end street."

Tony was about to explode. "You have to believe me!" he shouted.

"Calm down," said the editor, trying to get Tony to accept the situation. He tapped ashes from his cigar onto the floor, and then, lifting his cigar to his lips, he relit it using an old Zippo. Dejected, Tony walked toward the door. "You'll soon feel better," the editor called out. "Once you get your fat check for the photos of Boyce Belder's corpse."

Unconcerned with money at this point, Tony went out the door, strolling slowly off, sad and disillusioned. When he reached the street, he was surprised to see Doreen standing on the corner, casually observing automobile traffic passing through the intersection.

Tony approached her. "Doreen?" he asked, uncertain it was really her. "Is it you?"

"Oh, Tony," she said. "Yeah, it's me."

"What are doing here?" Tony asked.

Doreen nervously fluffed her hair. "I guess I came here to find you," she replied.

Tony cocked an eye and gazed inquiringly at her. "You mean you don't know for sure?" he asked, puzzled by her reply. "How'd you know I'd be here?"

Doreen ran her fingers through the curls of her hair. "I'm not sure," she answered.

"You're not sure!" Tony forcefully echoed.

"No," replied Doreen.

Tony sighed sharply. Then he walked toward his Firebird. Doreen ran to catch up to him. "Where are we going?" she asked, trying to stay in step.

"No place," Tony replied stoically.

"We have to be going somewhere, don't we?" Doreen wondered.

Tony stopped in his tracks, and he scratched his head while considering the question. Seeing a park bench across the street, he rambled over to it. Sitting down, he rested his head in his hands.

Doreen approached and stood beside the bench. "Who's the person you're thinking about?" she asked out of nowhere.

Tony peered inquisitively. "What makes you think I'm thinking about somebody?" he asked.

Doreen blinked her eyes, seemingly vexed by Tony. "Well, you are, aren't you?"

Tony stood up, and surrendering himself to Doreen, he motioned for her to follow him. "We're going to take a drive," he told her. "Up to Ventura."

"Why Ventura?"

"I got to visit somebody."

"Who?"

"Somebody I should have visited a long time ago."

Tony and Doreen traveled up the Pacific Coast passing through miles of scenery. They mentioned nothing about its beauty though, but simply rode in the brightness of the noonday sunshine, the Firebird gliding in warm silence. They navigated their way into the town of Ventura and arrived to a place that appeared to be a school. It was secured by a stone wall and a wrought-iron gate, but the gate was open, and Tony drove through it. Doreen noticed a sign that read *Los Padres Orphanage*. She peered about its grounds, noticing it was full of fruit trees and gardens.

Tony parked the Firebird at the curb of the entrance to the orphanage, and he went inside while Doreen remained in the car. Rambling up to the reception desk, he asked to see Padre Marquez.

The receptionist was a mature woman who spoke graciously. "I'm sorry," she said softly. "Padre Marquez is no longer with us."

Tony was disappointed. "Where'd he go?" he asked. "I'd like to find him."

"That won't be possible," the receptionist answered. "He passed away a year ago." Tony's face fell, and he was obviously wounded.

The receptionist tried to cheer him up. "Padre Marquez left something for you," she said smiling. "He left something for all his children who return to visit." Reaching into a drawer of her desk, she withdrew an envelope and handed it to Tony. "This is for you."

Accepting the envelope, Tony turned aside and mopped off down the hallway. Walking outdoors, he meandered passed his Firebird. Finding a shady tree, he leaned against its truck. He opened the envelope, and he discovered a letter was inside.

"My Dear Children," the letter began. "I'm delighted that you returned to visit me. I'm sorry I'm not there to greet you in person, but I've passed from your world, and I have entered another. Please, don't be sad, for I lived a good life. It was wonderful to be your guardian. I take with me into eternity many fond memories. I always enjoyed seeing your lovely faces, and also hearing your charming voices, which were sometimes boisterous, but they were music to my ears. There's so much I want to tell you, but I cannot find the words to convey my thoughts. Life is sometimes difficult, and yet, it is also a beautiful thing. Be diligent, abide with hope, and have compassion for one another. A pure heart prevails over all obstacles. Remember me with fondness, knowing you always brought my life great joy."

A teardrop fell from Tony's cheek, and he quickly wiped it away by a brush of his hand. He noticed that Doreen now stood before him.

"Are you okay?" she asked.

"Yeah, sure," Tony replied.

"What does the letter say?"

"Nothing much."

Doreen removed the letter from his hands, and he allowed her to do so. After she read the letter, she handed it back to him. "I didn't know you lived in an orphanage."

"You never asked."

"Padre Marquez was a nice person. I understand why you feel so bad."

"It's more than that," Tony explained. "I wanted him to be proud of me. I wanted him to know that I'd be somebody—not just a photojournalist for a sleazy tabloid, but a real journalist, one who writes stories." Tony fell deep into grief. "But it's too late now."

"It's not too late," Doreen said. "I'm sure he's looking down from above. You can still make him proud. You can still become a writer—a good one."

"Doreen, you don't understand," Tony said. "The Exploiter didn't want my story. If they don't want my stuff, I'm sure nobody else will. Besides, I got nothing interesting to write about."

"Sure you do," said Doreen. "You can write about everything that happened to us when we were with Josh and his bother Boyce."

Tony rubbed his temples with the palms of his hands. "You mean like when Boyce Belder turned into a wild beast," he said glibly. "And Josh Belder blew his head off."

Doreen shrugged. "Well, yeah," she said meekly.

"I'd rather not be reminded," Tony commented.

"Then you could write about when I was with Boyce Belder. We were in his Ferrari driving through the desert and going two-hundred miles an hour. He was laughing and talking crazy, saying things like he can feel the earth's power. He tried to reach inside my blouse, but I wouldn't let him."

"Did that really happen?" Tony asked surprised.

"Yeah, and other things too," Doreen declared.

"Like what?" Tony quizzed.

"Don't you remember?" Doreen asked.

"Just tell me," Tony requested.

"You and me and Josh were in Los Angeles in my little car," Doreen began. "The police were chasing us. Josh told me to turn into a garage and drive up to the roof. Then he told me to drive my car over the edge. He said that everything would be okay, so I did it. We vanished into thin air, and the next thing we know we're in Malibu, rolling with the surf on the beach."

"Yeah, I kind of do remember that," said Tony, thinking back. "It does sound like an interesting story."

"You could write a whole book about everything that happened," Doreen said excitedly. "It could be an adventure novel."

"Look, Doreen, I can't write a novel," Tony confessed. "I ain't smart enough. Writing novels is for guys who got education."

Tony trudged off toward his Firebird, and Doreen followed him.

"I can help you," Doreen said, encouraging Tony. "I went to college some."

"I don't know," Tony responded reluctantly. "Writing a novel is a big deal."

Tony opened the door to his car and slipped into the driver seat. He watched as Doreen got in the passenger side. Folding her hands in her lap, she sat calmly.

"Where are we going?" she asked.

"Why do you always ask me that?" Tony shot back.

"Because everybody's always going somewhere," she replied. "I told you that already."

Tony was near his wit's end, but he remained composed. "I'm going back to Los Angeles," he said. "To my apartment and get some rest. I feel like I haven't slept in a week."

"I'll go with you," said Doreen. "I'll stay at your place."

"You wanna stay at my place?"

"Is it okay?"

"I don't think I have much of a choice."

"I guess not."

"That's what I figured."

"We're in this together," Doreen conveyed. "You, me and Josh Belder."

"Josh Belder? Didn't he vanish?"

Doreen nervously fluffed her hair. "Yeah, but some people just seem to show up anyplace."

Tony inserted a key into the ignition of the Firebird. "I know somebody like that," he said, glancing askance at Doreen.

"Who's that?" Doreen asked.

Tony cranked the engine of the Firebird and pulled away from the curb. "You're really something, Doreen. You're really something."

Doreen did not respond, but merely stared out the window of the Firebird, peering off toward the vastness of the faraway unknown.

SALVAGERS

"Salvagers" is a story of humor. It indicates the author's interest in a wide range of genres in short-fiction.

She was haggard and he was bent, the couple who traversed the affluent neighborhood in the town of Smithville. He had tattoos on his arms and neck, and she had a scar at the corner of her forehead. He wore faded overalls with tattered straps. She wore baggy jeans held up by a belt decorated with rhinestones. He covered his head with a baseball cap, tightly wearing it to keep his dishwater hair running the length of his back. She dyed her hair red, and fixed it with a grubby visor.

The couple were poor folks who did what they could in the face of circumstance. Some might call them trash-pickers, though no one in town used such harsh words to reference them. Most people referred to them as *those people*, or *the Buzbees*, for that in fact was their name, Mandolyn and Casper-Roy. As far as the Buzbees were concerned, their occupation was within the broad industry of salvage, and while the term salvage was not refined in connotation, it was somewhat pliable to the ear, and the Buzbees liked it, calling themselves *salvagers*.

Affluent people in town found it inconceivable that a couple could make a living by picking trash, but the Buzbees managed to do it. The trick was in knowing the value of things, like small appliances, knickknacks, toys and even books. Books were something new to the Buzbees, for they had only recently found a decent one. They tried it out on a second-hand bookseller. The result was good, for they had sold it for fifty dollars. So with memory of that success lingering in their minds, they rummaged through heaps of trash in the hope of another rich discovery.

Jacquelyn Saint Jean, a reclusive, parsimonious widow, lived in a grand Victorian-style house on the cul-de-sac of Carolina Court. Her husband had passed on a few years ago, and feeling that the house had become too much for her, she considered selling the place. She invested an entire weekend in cleaning out her garage, and by late afternoon on Sunday, she had amassed a mammoth mound of refuse for Monday morning pick up. Seeing the trash on the curb of her home, Ms. Saint Jean found it an excruciating eye-sore. She was delighted when night fell and shadowed the awful pile. In the morning, though, daylight once again illuminated the trash. The widow peered anxiously through the blinds of her library window, waiting for the truck to arrive and take the refuse away.

Trash, however, is like beauty—it's in the eye of the beholder, and when the Buzbees' eyes lit upon Ms. Saint Jean's refuse, they considered it exquisite. Pulling up to the curb in an old station wagon, the Buzbees stepped out sprightly. They soon salvaged a hard-wood stool, a compact microwave, and a transistor radio, which wasn't worth much, but it had a fine appearance, and Casper-Roy figured its condition would augment its value. Then he saw something quite special. He reached his rough-knuckled hand into a box of magazines and lifted out a hardcover book. Mandolyn, seeing the book in his hands, smiled broadly, the gaps of her teeth coming into full view. She took the book from her husband's hands and thumbed through its pages, barely able to keep from giggling. Inserting the book inside her belt, she pulled her shirt down over it, making sure it was safe and secure.

Curtis Darlane, a semi-retired schoolteacher, was proprietor of Smithville's only used bookstore. Each month Curtis invited an author in from the city to give a reading and to have coffee with customers. When the Buzbees pulled into the bookstore parking lot, Curtis was setting out cups and saucers for an event. His customers, each of them delectably intellectual, noticed the Buzbees approach the bookstore's entrance, and a detached silence came over them.

"I'll take care of this," Curtis told his clients. "Excuse me a moment."

Curtis met the Buzbees at the door and hampered their entrance. Pushing his hair back behind his ears, he softly asked, "what do you have for me?"

Mandolyn withdrew the book from beneath her blouse, and she handed it over. Curtis needed but a fraction of a second to appraise it.

"It's worth nothing to me," he said.

Casper-Roy was stunned voiceless, but not Mandolyn. "Why is this one worth nothin' when the other was worth fifty dollars?" she asked vociferously.

"Look, I'll give you a dollar for it," Curtis said, reaching into his pocket.

The offer irritated Casper-Roy. "We spent more than that on gas gettin' over here," he complained. "A dollar's an insult."

"I'm sorry," Curtis said, handing the book back. "I wish it were worth more, but it's not."

Casper-Roy saw fire building in his wife's eyes. Wanting to avoid a crisis, he intervened with a soothing comment. "We understand," he said. "Some books are better than others, like everything else in the world."

He tried to pull Mandolin away, but she continued to glare at Curtis, her gaze framing him in disdain. "So's we don't waste yours and ours time," she said. "Tell us what books are worth somethin' and which ones ain't."

Curtis was cavalier. "I haven't time now," he conveyed. "Come by tomorrow and we'll talk." Turning on his heels, left the Buzbees to make their exit. Assuming an elevated spot at the front of the bookstore, he introduced the topic for the day's event. "Our author will discuss southern fiction," he stated. "And how important it is in Modern Literature."

Mandolyn cocked an eye. "Ain't that the name of our book, Casper-Roy?" she asked. "Southern Fiction?"

Inspecting the title of the book, Casper-Roy nodded his head in agreement. "Sure is," he said.

"This here Curtis fella is trying to rob us," Mandolyn declared. "He knows we got talent for findin' books, and he's plannin' on buyin' them, but for little nothin'."

Mandolyn's instincts compelled her to confront Curtis, but Casper-Roy held her back. "We'll take care of this tomorrow," he said.

Casper-Roy then led Mandolyn out the door and ushered her toward their station wagon.

About that wagon. It was a vintage 78 model Caprice, beige in color with red vinyl interior, fold-down rear seats, white-wall tires, and a chrome roof rack. A big V8 under the hood made the wagon a roadster on the highway, but it was a gas guzzler around town. The Buzbees, though, rarely drove more than thirty miles per hour, for the wagon was usually weighted down with cargo, and with its rear shocks blown out, it tended to bounce and bump. Nevertheless, the Caprice was dependable, and it never let the Buzbees down, except for an occasional flat tire.

As the Buzbees traveled along, Casper-Roy noticed that Mandolyn still stewed with anger. "Try an' look on the bright side," he said, wanting to cheer up his wife. "We had a good day of salvagin'."

Mandolin desired to relax, but she couldn't. She leaned back in her seat, and folding her arms across her chest, she tightened her lips. "I ain't forgettin' about that bookstore fella," she said tersely. "I'm gonna make sure that Curtis fella treats us right."

Drops of rain fell from the sky, and Casper-Roy flipped on the wagon's windshield wipers. They made a screeching sound against the glass, but he ignored the noise. Mandolyn closed her eyes and attempted to nap. Curtis remained on her mind, however, and she could only sit back alert, anxiously waiting for the big wagon to arrive home.

Buzbee house was a weathered tract home built some time mid-century. Although an adequate shelter, sections of it were no longer functional. The concrete floor of the porch was busted and cracked. The one-car garage was detached and lopsided, the sun having shrunk it into disparate angles. The lawn was over-grown with weeds, and an old pecan tree hung above the house with broken limbs.

When the Buzbees arrived, the rain was coming down in sheets, and Casper-Roy had to hustle to bring a few salvaged items into the house for inspection. Mandolyn went directly inside, and seeing the ceiling was leaking, she placed a two-gallon pot on the floor to catch the falling water. The moment Casper-Roy came in the front door, she unburdened her mind. "I don't trust him none," she said, referring to Curtis. "Some folks try to cheat ya at every turn. It's a shame 'cause we might could make a fortune with all the books we can get our hands on."

Casper-Roy set down the compact microwave he brought in, and he gave it a cursory inspection. It was exceptionally clean, which was a good sign, for it meant its prior owner had cared for it. "It's the same ole story," he said, responding to his wife. "Poor folks do all the work, and rich folks get all the money." He pushed a button on the microwave and gave it a ten-second test. "Rich folks got more education than poor folks," he added. "So they got the advantage."

Mandolyn partially agreed. "Yeah, but times are changin'," she said. "Poor folks can learn more stuff. There's computers nowadays."

Casper-Roy listened to the hum of the microwave and was convinced the machine worked okay. "What are you sayin',

Mandolyn?" he asked, irritated by his wife's remarks. "You think I should learn the fixin' of computers?"

"No, Casper-Roy," she replied. "I'm talkin' about the internet. That's where ever'body learns things. Barb Thompson's boy, Jimmy, he was dim-witted, but he knows about the internet and now he's a computer genius. I'm thinkin' of going down to her place and learning some about our southern fiction book. That way, tomorrow when we see Curtis, we'll know what is, and what's not."

Mandolyn thoughtfully massaged her chin with her knuckles. After a long moment, she opened the living-room closet door and removed a windbreaker jacket.

"Where you goin'?" asked Casper-Roy.

"Down to Barb Thompson's place," Mandolyn replied.

"In the rain?" he asked. "You goin' out in the rain?"

"Yeah," she replied. "Better gettin' wet than robbed."

A platinum blond divorcee with two teenage children, Barb Thompson lived around the corner from the Buzbees. Barb and Mandolyn were friends, often drinking coffee and gossiping while doing laundry together.

When Mandolyn knocked on her friend's door, Trisha, Barb's eldest child, answered. "Hi. Mrs. Buzbee," said the high-school senior. Although she wore wire-rim glasses, Trisha was cute when wearing low-cut jeans and tight blouses. "My mama's in the kitchen."

Mandolyn walked dripping wet through the living room and passed into the kitchen where Barb was cleaning up.

"Good to see ya," said Barb, greeting her friend. "Let me take that wet jacket." She took the jacket from Mandolyn, and she tossed it into the dryer. "You want a cup of coffee?"

Mandolyn accepted, and after Barb filled a pair of cups with black liquid, the two friends sat down for a chat.

"What brings you out in the rain?" Barb asked. "Casper-Roy been misbehaving?"

"No," replied Mandolyn. "I came by 'cause I need your boy to get me somethin' off the internet."

"Billy!" Barb shouted into the other room. "Come on in here."

An unruly eighth-grader, Billy spent most on his time playing video games. "I'm busy!" he shouted back.

Trisha entered the kitchen. "Mama, you know Billy. He won't move when he's playing a game."

"Well, tell him to get in here," Barb demanded. "Mandolyn needs some help with the internet."

"What do you need, Mrs. Buzbee?" Trisha asked. "I'll help you with it."

"I thought Billy was the computer genius in the family," Mandolyn commented.

"He's no genius," Trisha retorted. "He's just my dumb brother."

Mandolyn grinned with amusement. "Okay, Trisha," she said. "I wanna know something about this book I got. It's called *Southern Fiction*."

Trisha paused, carefully considering Ms. Buzbees' request. "Southern fiction isn't a book title," she said. "It's a genre."

"A what?" asked Mandolyn.

"Some authors write romance books, and others write mysteries," Trisha explained. "Many authors from the south write southern fiction."

"Well, okay," Mandolyn glossing over her gaffe. "Find me some famous names of southern fiction writers."

Trisha obeyed and went into the den where she sat down at here computer. She promptly returned with a printout of southern fiction writers. "Here's a list," she announced. "Some of the writers I recognize from English class. I'm sure most of them are famous."

Mandolyn scrutinized the list. "So these writers are best sellers," she surmised. "Looks like most are in the book we got.

Now I know for sure that bookstore fella's trying to cheat us. He offered us a dollar for a book that's probably worth a hundred."

"Where'd you get the book?" asked Barb.

"We salvaged it from a rich widow over on Carolina Court," Mandolyn replied.

"I know her," said Trisha. "Her name is Jacquelyn Saint Jean. She was an English teacher last year at school. All the kids used to talk about her, saying she was mean and crazy.

"Is she mean and crazy?" asked Barb.

"No, Mama," replied Trish. "She's a sensitive woman, and she loves literature. I learned a lot in her class." Trisha thought back to her prior year in high school. "She didn't let the boys get away with any crap, though. I wish she'd come back to school, but I don't think she will, not with all the gossip about her murderin' her husband."

"She killed her husband?" Barb asked aghast.

"No, Mama," Trisha replied. "But when the boys in class misbehaved, she'd give them an evil eye, and it was really scary."

The next morning, the Buzbees arose early and had a breakfast of sausage and biscuits. The rain had quit sometime during the night, but a heavy layer of water still clung to the windows of the Caprice. Casper-Roy had to use a towel to wipe the glass clean, and when he was finished, he hopped in the wagon and cranked its engine. Mandolyn heard the roar of the big V8, and she strutted out of the house. Stepping into the car, she pulled the door shut with a slam.

Curtis intuited that the Buzbees might arrive early, and the first thing he did after opening the bookstore was make a pot of hot coffee and set out fresh pastry. Despite the warm reception, Mandolyn was cool toward Curtis.

"Okay, fella," she said, biting into an apple tart. "We're here and we're listenin'."

Curtis motioned for the Buzbees to cross over to a table where he had laid out a pair of books, which appeared similar, but they were quite different. He opened one of the books and pointed to a page. "You see," he said, encouraging the Buzbees to take a close look. "This book is special and quite valuable. It's a first edition. It says so right here, *first edition.*"

The Buzbees hovered over the page and inspected it. "We can read," Mandolyn said snidely. "We ain't dummies."

Curtis lifted the other book. "There's nothing special about this book. It's in its fifth printing. It can be purchased for a few dollars." The bookseller feigned to smile. "The book you brought me last week is a first edition, and its author is *Flannery O'Connon.*"

Mandolyn's hands fell from her hips, and Curtis believed he'd successfully smoothed the woman's feathers. However, she began to chime. "Our book is sure worth more than one dang dollar."

Curtis ruminated for moment. "Okay," he said. "I'll give you three dollars for it."

Mandolin reinserted the book under her belt and pulled her shirt down over it. "Naa," she muttered. "We'll hold on to it."

Once the Buzbees were outdoors, Casper-Roy expressed his opinion. "We should've took that three dollars," he said. "It would have paid for our gas gettin' over here."

"You didn't see what I seen," Mandolyn shot back. "That book we sold Curtis for fifty dollars, he's got under glass for five hundred."

"I'll be durn," Casper-Roy responded. "We'll have to be smarter next time."

"Yeah, said Mandolyn," a devious glint in her eyes. "And I got us a plan."

"What?—what you got in mind?" Casper-Roy asked, almost afraid to learn the answer.

"I'm thinking 'bout that widow on Carolina Court," she replied. "I bet ya she's got lots of books. Maybe she got some first editions she don't know about. We can buy some of her books and sell 'em to Curtis for a good profit."

Casper-Roy was impressed. "Okay," he said. "Let's go see the widow."

Ms. Saint Jean's grand Victorian-style house appeared to scintillate with the mist of morning, the sun beaming silvery rays between the pickets of her fence, like a row of lighthouses. Inside the house, Ms. Saint Jean washed dishes following a breakfast of berries, toast, and marmalade. The doorbell rang, and she answered it without bothering to look through the peep hole. When she opened the door, her spirit fell out of her soul, for standing on the porch were *those people*. Dumbfounded, she was unable to ask what they wanted.

Mandolyn, however, was able to speak with great ease. "We come here to talk business," she said, inching inside the door.

Stunned by the woman's words, Ms. Saint Jean did nothing to stop her. *What kind of business could these people possibly have with me?* she asked herself. She noticed the big Caprice wagon on the curb, and she became impacted with the fact that the Buzzes— devoted trash pickers, were inside her house. She considered rushing to the phone and dialing the police, but if the Buzbees chose to fight, she'd be no match against them.

"We're interested in buyin' some of your books," said Casper-Roy civilly.

Perhaps they're harmless, Ms. Saint Jean now thought. "Books?" she asked aloud. "Did you say books?"

"Yeah," Mandolyn replied. "We're in the buyin' and sellin' business, and we're lookin' to buy some books."

The foyer led to the widow's library, and Casper-Roy peeked inside it. "You mind if we take a take a look at your books?" he asked.

"Well," Ms. Saint Jean replied uneasily. "I guess, perhaps, it will be okay." She allowed the Buzbees to enter the library, and they meandered about as if inside a great hall of records.

"Maybe I can help you," the widow suggested.

"We're lookin' for first editions," Caper-Roy responded. "That's what collectors are buyin'."

Mandolyn stepped on her husband's foot to shut him up.

Ms. Saint Jean was amused, and she pressed her fingers to her lips to conceal her mirth. "I certainly wouldn't be interested in selling any first editions," she explained. "I'm a collector myself." With a sweep of her hand, she ushered the Buzbees out of the library. The Buzbees had little recourse but to follow the widow through the foyer and back onto the porch. "Kindly wait here a moment," Ms. Saint Jean requested. "I have something I'd like to give you."

Before the Buzbees could stop her, the widow went inside the house and shut the door. Mandolyn gave Casper-Roy a look of disgust, and it spoke to him with expletives.

The widow reappeared and addressed the Buzbees. "Here's something for you to read," she said, handing Mandolyn a book. "It's not a first edition, but it's very good reading." The widow smiled graciously. "You'll find something inside for your trouble," she added.

Mandolyn opened the book and saw a five-dollar bill. Casper-Roy reacted by snatching it and stuffing it into his pocket. "It'll pay for our gas comin' over," he said.

Satisfied, Ms. Saint Jean stepped back inside, but before closing the door, she looked back. "Should you find any first editions elsewhere," she announced. "You may stop by and inquire if I'like to the purchase the item. I'm a very generous buyer."

Lights went on inside Mandolyn's head. "How much you wanna give for Flannery O'Connor?" she asked.

Ms. Saint Jean contemplated, for she knew about the book in question. Curtis at the bookstore had telephoned her about it. He offered her the O'Connor for five-hundred dollars, which seemed a bit excessive, but she was considering it. "How much would it take to buy it?" asked the widow.

Mandolyn calculated a figure in her head. "You might could buy it for four-hundred dollars," she replied.

"If it's in excellent condition," said the widow. "I'll purchase the O'Connor."

Once Ms. Saint Jean disappeared, Casper-Roy bowed up to his wife. "That book ain't ours to sell," he said. "And that bookstore fella wants five-hundred for it. I don't see how you figure on doin' business."

Mandolyn tightened her rhinestone belt. "We're gonna negotiate," she said resolutely.

Twenty minutes later, the Buzbees entered the bookstore and found Curtis behind the counter, packing a box of books for a special delivery. Mandolyn charged directly up to him, not giving him the opportunity to properly greet her.

"We wanna buy ourselves that book we sold ya," she declared. "We expect you'll make a fair profit. But we're cash buyers, and we're ready to do business."

Curtis wasn't interested. "I've no obligation to sell," he said. "It's a first edition, and it's by Flannery O'Connor."

"Name your price," Mandolyn responded. "And we'll buy that fella's book from ya."

"Her book," Curtis said curtly. "Flannery O'Connor is a woman."

The Buzzbees exchanged furtive glances. "Whatever," said Mandolyn. "Just tell us what you want for it.'"

Curtis considered the proposition carefully. "I've already had some interest from collectors," he began. "They feel that five-hundred dollars is a reasonable figure. However, given the circumstance of your having brought the book to my attention, I'm willing to sell it to you for four-hundred."

Casper-Roy was obliged to speak. "That's a three-hundred and fifty-dollar profit," he said, awed by the amount. "And for doin' little nothing."

Curtis didn't trouble himself with an explanation.

Mandolyn whispered to Casper-Roy. "How much cash we got?" she asked.

Casper-Roy withdrew an Indian billfold from his back pocket, and opening it, he thumbed though its contents. "Looks to be three-hundred," he replied.

Posed in a business-like manner, Mandolyn addressed Curtis. "Our offer is three hundred," she declared. "Cash on the barrelhead."

Curtis resigned himself to the proposal, for if he didn't, the Buzbees would continue to prod him, and he would waste his day dealing with them. "Very well," he said. "I accept your offer of three-hundred dollars."

Meanwhile on Carolina Court, Ms. Saint Jean telephoned her gardener, James, a stalwart Afro-American, and she summoned him to her house. *I know how to handle those people,* she said to herself as she hung up the phone...

When the Buzbees returned to the widow's house, they found James on the front lawn trimming the hedges with a pair of shears. His eyes followed them intrepidly as they strolled up the walkway.

"I don't like how that fella is watching us," said Casper-Roy rambling beside his wife. "Looks like a killer to me."

"Don't mind him none," Mandolyn instructed. "We come here for business, and we ain't gonna cause no trouble."

Ms. Saint Jean watched from a window, waiting for the Buzbees to reach the door. Therefore, when the Buzbees rang the doorbell, she responded promptly.

"Please, come in," she said. "Let's go into the library." The widow gestured for the Buzbees to sit on a love seat, while she remained standing, anxious to see the O'Connor.

Mandolyn proudly handed her the book. "Take a look."

Ms. Saint Jean examined it closely. "Yes, it's in good condition."

Mandolyn agreed. "Sure is, and if you got the four hundred in cash, you can put it up on the shelf."

The time came for the widow to act. "Yes, I'd love to," she began melodiously. "But I'm alone, and my finances are limited. Books are so important to me. I recall my childhood in Savannah. My dear father adored books. He would read me stories as we sat together on the porch. I have such fond memories." The widow lingered in the center of the room, fluttering her eyelids and languidly floating about. She glanced down at the Buzbees, trying to determine if she had won their sympathy.

Casper-Roy whispered to his wife. "This widow woman must be crazy."

Mandolyn shifted in her seat and crossed her legs. "Like a fox maybe."

"My father passed away while I was still a child," the widow went on. "On his deathbed he asked me to save his library. He hoped it would one day have the finest books of southern fiction." She clutched a dainty a kerchief and held it sadly to her face. "It's all I have to remember my father."

"We all got sad stories," Mandolyn said. "My old man was a drunk, and Casper-Roy's daddy died in prison."

Ms. Saint Jean was in a quandary, and yet she was determined to play her drama through to the end. She crossed over to a bookshelf, and she ran her fingers over the bindings of a row books. "I recall the jasmines in bloom, their sweet fragrance in the air. Oh, such wonderful memories. Flannery O'Connor, I miss you...."

Mandolyn turned to her husband, and raising her eyebrows, she said in a low whisper, "I think she's negotiating." Levering herself off the love seat, she address the widow with authority. "Ain't nobody can change the past. Things happen. Ain't no one to blame. That's the way life is and always gonna be." The widow was taken aback, and Mandolyn continued to push. "Now, you said you'd give four-hundred dollars for the O'Connor book. That's what you said, and that's what's you gotta do."

Ms. Saint Jean hadn't anticipated such audacity, and it enraged her. She marched to the front door, and opening it, she tersely called out. "Come in, James! I've completed my business with *those people!*"

James stepped inside and stood in the foyer, his large body looming menacingly.

The widow disappeared inside the house, and James remained behind, his gaze boring into the Buzbees like a pair of murderous drills. The widow reappeared with her purse. She opened it, and withdrawing an envelope, she countered out three-hundred and fifty dollars. "This is all you get!" the widow cried out. "Take it or leave it! I'd just as soon negotiate with Curtis than do business with you!"

Casper-Roy turned to Mandolyn, his eyes asking what he should do. "Take the dang money," she declared. "And let's get out of here."

Casper-Roy stuffed the cash into his billfold, and he bustled outdoors with Mandolyn.

"Don't say nothin'!" Mandolyn sounded off. "And gimme the dang keys to the wagon. I'm' drivin'!"

Mandolyn furiously cranked the Caprice. Dropping it into gear, she screeched away from the curb. The wagon sped through the neighborhood until it arrived to a place where police often lay in wait for speeders. Mandolyn slowed the machine into a smooth glide. After a few minutes of gliding, Mandolyn regained her composure.

"That widow was some kind of nut. We had no choice but to take the three-fifty. She might have gone bananas if we didn't."

Casper-Roy figured it was okay to speak. "Least ways we made fifty dollars, plus the five she give us. That makes fifty-five. Not bad for a couple hours work," He noticed the book the widow had given them. It laid on the seat between him and Mandolyn. He lifted the book and flipped though its pages. "And we also got this book." he added. "Maybe I'll do some readin' of it."

Mandolin grabbed the book from Casper-Roy's hands, and she tossed it into the back of the wagon. "Don't bother."

"Why not?"

"Book-reading drives folks crazy."

The wagon disappeared into traffic. Casper-Roy laid his head in the palms of his hands. Mandolyn relaxed behind the wheel, and she hummed a few bars of a Neil Young song. Life began to feel right again. However, she knew her world was different now. She and Casper-Roy would never be the same, for from this day forward, they would be uncommon salvagers.

PART THREE: EARLY POEMS

The poems "Paradise," "Goddess," and "Soliloquy" are taken from a larger narrative drafted circa 1980. The poems "Discourse on Beauty," "Slave," and "For Professor" (note 8) were written at different times between 1978 and 1982.

PARADISE

Only the birds of paradise sing
When beyond the garden that lady is passing,
And I, a lord, once her lover am watching
From the story terrace the sky filtering
Her light we are one thought.
And she is passing, the eye agleam,
Hair shimmering, the silver shoulder seems
Like a polite wave on the open sea.
Now in the darkness her light reveals
The folded petals of sleeping flowers,
Like gems for the nightly hours.
Beyond my terrace-seat she slips,
Like she were a moon with heaven's secret.
Now for an urgent moment is set
Naked where ghostly lovers stretch
On the sky's gray softness.
Now the darkness, the garden's awaiting
That lady, that lady.

GODDESS

Now the way of life is the sky,
Stars the gates that unlock the soul,
Their bodies large, like workmen strong,
Rise up unbound to push beyond.
I am a light, shameless and once
A lover of lords are lights of old,
But now a lady gone from them
Who bade me sheet the mortal with cold.
I am a bed of thoughtful souls.
My softness has arranged them,
To lie where Gods once were drawn,
To watch my silver dress unloose
The fire they fall in to love.
And mortals now out on the sky
All are strong with dreams of light,
And I their Goddess love them,
And in portions above world, glow,
And in loveliness sing,
And aloft among stars, dream,
And reposed in a garden among flowers,
I enchant them with a heavenly purpose.
To guide the circuits of heaven am I,
Now the way of life is the sky.

SOLILOQUY

I did not know what beauty was here,
On the grassy tiers grown over with clover,
And the air's flowery sweetness, which gives
My thoughts a moment away from themselves,
But now I know the grounded loveliness,
And why men live their lives to heir large lots of it.
Yet more than a garden is their home,
For what are with light is to spin
Among the stars never separate from them.
But unto the moon they thoughtless dive,
And among gray collections of ash they lay
Like a fire's late-night embers
Slowly dying with the coming of day.

FOR PROFESSOR

The following poem (note 8) was written for Doctor Paul Gray, a former Professor of Speech at the University of Texas.

When I read upon lines you said
Should be heard, should be read
As if a voice were singing clear',
I too often fear how label,
Although I hear and wish myself
Enabled with a scholar's terms.
Yet I grow tired when I try learn.
Yes, my dilemma is true,
For I have hope to learn from you,
But terms drive me to craz',
And perhaps I am a bit too laz',
Yet I have heard rhythms beat,
Have had my own hand defeat a rhyme
By laying awkward on the line,
And I have had my own head pained
By reading over the words that came,
And remembered how difficult it is,
To have them fit so they might live
Labeled by that man's scope, poetry I hope.

DISCOURSE ON BEAUTY

There are secrets divine that tell
Of lovely forms which in waters dwell,
And ride the waves enchanted at sea,
And bind our eyes to beauty with dreams.
And there are sounds lovely,
Songs so perfect the spirit feels
Transit with immortal wills,
Which sirens fix from windy hills.
And there are philosophies lovely,
Ideas inspired in youth and passion,
Uniting truth and beauty in reams of poetry.
And where beauty sits sofas seem as sea,
A voice the sound of heavenly melody,
An idea the work of philosophy mused,
She is a song, a secret, and truth.
And to see her one with oceans dream,
Hear her voice one the heavens share,
Know her thoughts wisdom is revealed,
And to love her now all beauty becomes real.

SLAVE

I am a slave to old powers,
And cannot rest except to sleep,
Though here, too, my master seeks me.
And in my cell of dreams invades
The sole freedom the hours make
And over my unknowing bed teaches:
What things the sages cannot say
And remain among the rest of us,
For what forms therein, words cannot express,
Cannot convey what aged powers imagine,
Not that which comes in dreams to create,
And with high images incarcerates
A slave who wished to flee his fate.

NOTES

1. Jack Shannon (no middle name) was raised in and around Mississippi and Louisiana until he was thirteen when he moved with his mother and three sisters to Houston, Texas. He attended Jeff Davis High School, and despite a deformed ankle, he played all-city basketball in 1939. A handsome, affable young man, he was well-liked by everyone who met him. When World War broke out he joined the army, and he earned many commendations for his service, including saving the life of a fellow soldier by carrying him down a shelled-out hill. At the end of the war, he met and married Margaret Morrison of Pennsylvania. They settled in Waco, Texas where Jack worked as a cotton buyer for a group of New York brokers. In 1953 the family moved to southeast Houston where Jack worked with a local cotton company until the late 1950's. During this period Jack began to exhibit symptoms of schizophrenia, and he was hospitalized with mental breakdowns on numerous occasions. The cause of his condition remains unknown. It may have been due to the trauma of war, his discontent with employers, or a stained relationship with his spouse. Whatever the reason, his emotional affliction stayed with him throughout his life. He passed way from this world at the age of eighty-four. The cause of his death was hemorrhaging of

the brain due to prolonged over-medication of prescription-drug blood thinners.

2. John Shannon, Jack's older brother, was a victim of his father's violent nature. The old man whipped John with a belt on quite a few occasions. When John became a bulky teenager, his father turned to beating him with his fist; that is until one day when John got the best of him. John welded a heavy stick and threatened to break his father's legs if he wouldn't cease his bullying. The father begged his son not to hurt him. But once John dropped his weapon, he lifted it up and beat his son violently. It was weeks before John recovered from his injuries. Leaving home at the age of fifteen, he vowed to never see his father again. He never did. He lived out his life alone in west Texas working the oil fields. A hermit, he saved nearly every dollar he earned. When he died at the age of seventy-five from a self-inflicted shotgun wound to the head, he bequeathed his estate worth nearly a million dollars to his brother and surviving sisters.

3. M.D. Shannon has been under the care of doctors at Liver Associates of Texas by Victor Ankoman-Sey, M.D. and Scott Vela, Ph.D. since 2004. He credits them with bringing him out of death's throes and into a revitalized existence. .

4. *In The Land Of Cane* is a fictional story. However, it is based on little-known facts regarding the unjust imprisonment of Afro-Americans following the Civil War. Only recently has the public been informed about such cruel practices during America's era of "neo-slavery". See Douglas Blackmon's 2008 Pulitzer-Prize winning work in non fiction titled *Slavery By Any Other Name* for more information on the subject.

5. Bayard Taylor, 1825 to 1878, was a distinguished author, poet, essayist and world traveler. He was born in Kennett Square, Pennsylvania, and a library there bears his name. Bayard Taylor

School operates as a public school in north Philadelphia. In the 1960's, it was a first-grade thru eight-grade school, but today it teaches elementary-age children.

6. Richard Howard earned his B.A. from Columbia University, and he later studied at the Sorbonne as a Fellow of the French Government. He has written more than ten volumes of poetry, numerous literary essays, and he has published over one-hundred translations. A former President of Pen American Center, he has been Poet Laureate of New York, Chancellor of The Academy of American Poets, and also Poetry Editor of The Paris Review. He has held teaching positions at The Whitney Humanities Center at Yale, at Columbia University, and also The University of Houston where he was instrumental in creating a world-class Graduate Writing Program. Although it is little-known, Howard was a member of the inner-circle of New York Beats, which later became one of the most important literary movements in modern literature. He had close associations with Allen Ginsburg, William Burroughs, and Jack Kerouac, all of whom made major contributions to American letters.

7. *Tales From The Snakeskin Journal* was first drafted circa 1996 as a novel. However, parts of it were lost, and it was adapted as a collection of inner-related short stories

8. *For Professor* is referenced in the non fiction story *Teachers* in this volume. The phrase "that man's scope" is borrowed from T.S. Eliot's poem *Ash Wednesday*.

Copies of this book are available through Barnes & Nobel, Amazon, and also at the publisher's website. Author-read audio recordings of selections from this book are available at mdshannon. org. The Author can be contacted at his website.